WHAT'S LEFT OUT

LITERATURE AND MEDICINE

Michael Blackie, Editor • Carol Donley and Martin Kohn, Founding Editors

What's Left Out

JAY BARUCH

❦

THE KENT STATE UNIVERSITY PRESS

Kent, Ohio

For Jen and Daniel

❦

"Satellites" is reprinted from *Canadian Medical Association Journal* June 14, 2011, 183(9), pp. 1057–1058. © Canadian Medical Association 2011. This work is protected by copyright and the reprinting of this story was with the permission of the Canadian Medical Association Journal (www.cmaj.ca) and Access Copyright. Any alteration of its content or further reproduction in any form whatsoever is strictly prohibited unless otherwise permitted by law.

Cataloging information for this title is available at the Library of Congress.

19 18 17 16 15   5 4 3 2 1

Contents

❧

Acknowledgments

⁓

Whenever people ask how I find time to write, my response often resembles an allergic reaction. I scratch my neck, choke on words, and mutter some silly nonsense. But the serious answer begins and ends with an extraordinary, understanding, and loving family: my wife, Jen, and my son, Daniel. Can I mention my love for them without sounding sappy? I don't care. Now is a good time and place to sap away. I feel confident posting a sign that states there is little sap beyond this point. Our two dogs are less forgiving. But through canine prowess, they often sensed when writing became a shell game with the muses, and hinted through dog-speak that maybe I should take a break and go for a walk, and why not bring along the poop bags while you're at it.

I'm forever grateful for the love and support of my parents, Mel and Lucy Baruch; my sister, Amy; and my niece, Michelle.

The stories in this collection accrued slowly over seven years. Jen is my first reader, and Madeleine Beckman has provided expert feedback on early drafts of most, if not all, of these stories. Individual works have benefited from various people who were generous with their time and keen with their feedback. At the risk of making an embarrassing omission, these people include, but aren't limited to, Marty Kohn, Joyce Griffin, Lynda Schor, Jason Hack, Barbara Sibbald, Amy Baruch, and Tom Chandler.

I appreciate the input from various editors who published these stories in better form than when they arrived in their inbox.

I consider myself fortunate to be part of a remarkable faculty in the Department of Emergency Medicine at Alpert Medical School at Brown University. We are led by our chairman, Dr. Brian Zink, who champions the arts and humanities as well as the sciences. He's been a vital reader for many of these stories.

I'd be remiss if I didn't recognize immensely talented colleagues at the Cogut Center for the Humanities and the Granoff Center at Brown University. They have influenced and inspired my work in ill-defined but profound ways.

A special thanks goes to Michael Blackie, Will Underwood, Joyce Harrison, Rebekah Cotton, Mary Young, Susan Cash, and the editors and staff at Kent State University Press. I'm forever grateful to Carol Donley and Martin Kohn for their big hearts, wisdom, and early support.

These stories are fiction. The characters and events are narrative constructions. Resemblances or similarities to actual people or concrete events are coincidental, while setting some stories in unfamiliar and unsettling moral universes are deliberate.

Writers often have in mind particular readers whose opinions matter deeply. Sadly, two of these people, Walter James Miller and Jared Sable, have passed away since the publication of my first book. Each man was a renegade and uncompromising lover of the arts. The world is more conventional and less interesting without them.

These stories appeared in different forms in the following print and online journals:

"Avignon," *Tattoo Highway*

"Comfortable," "What's Left Out," and "Open Ended," *Hamilton Stone Review*

"Empowerment Center," *The Battered Suitcase*

"Fortunata" and "The Telephone Pole," *Bryant Literary Review*

"Rainbow," *Academic Emergency Medicine*

"Satellites," *Canadian Medical Association Journal*

"Soft Landings," *Eclectica Magazine*

"Sunday Night," and "Calling the Code," *Ars Medica*

1

Satellites

They roamed the University Hospital parking garage in search of his mother's Volvo wagon. "The next level," she insisted.

"We're at the top, Mom. The very top," he said.

He bristled and nodded, his teeth chattering. Each new level brought hope to her voice and confidence to her stride. By the time they spotted the car on the roof, alone, under stars and lamplight, the frozen gusts had needled his face raw.

"I knew she was hiding up here," she said.

"Let me drive. Your head's somewhere else."

"My head's right where it ought to be," his mother said, feverishly digging through her handbag. She couldn't find her keys. Defeat darkened her tired face, then embarrassment worked its way in. He leaned on the hood, arms crossed. His good luck sweater, roll-neck and stretched sleeves, labored a valiant but pitiful defense against winds that whipped a paper cup silly.

"No coat?" she said. "Would you let the kids come east in February without proper coats?"

"Cardiac surgery is an indoor sport," he said. "I assumed we'd be in the hospital, at home, or *inside the car.*"

"Very good. Pick on me, go ahead."

He gazed at the sky, sighed apologetically. The stars spread across the cloudless night like shattered glass. Her misremembering worried him.

"Ma, maybe the keys are in your hand," he suggested softly.

"Do I seem that dense to you?"

She turned her back to him before he could answer, unfurled each finger clenching her handbag. She drew that short breath he knew too well, that intake of exasperation. "Go ahead," she said. "Say something smart."

"Let's get in the car."

She unlocked the doors. A pause of unspoken forgiveness passed between them while she fumbled the key into the ignition. He blasted the heat.

"Dad's going to be fine," he hymned.

"I know," she said, a tinny amen.

His father had just received two new heart valves in surgery that stretched into evening. Afterward, caution creased the surgeon's face. Unexpected challenges presented themselves, he said. His mother blinked unemotionally as he described the surprisingly weak and flabby heart, the stress and extra work of adapting to new but unforgiving valves that no longer allowed blood to escape backward. "The next twenty-four hours will tell us where we're heading," the surgeon said. "Go home. Get some sleep."

They descended to level five, one floor below. Curved arrows in the pavement marked the exit ramp, but she kept missing the turn that would lead them down.

"Turn here," he said as they passed the exit a third time.

"The signs should be larger," she said, staring at her dashboard.

"Try looking up. It's called situational awareness."

"I'm aware. Very aware." She turned quickly to prove her point, only it returned them to the top level. He squeezed his scalp. Blood drummed into his ears.

"Where are you going? Turn around. Please."

She thumbed at the "No entry" sign back over her shoulder on the upward ramp.

"It's after midnight. There is nobody here."

"What if somebody thinks 5:00 P.M. is a good time to ignore a sign, or picking up their kid on-time from school justifies breaking the law? The strength of your beliefs doesn't make something right."

"This is not the time to play nice," he snapped.

They inched along the top level, as if exploring this terrain for the first time.

He caught her spying the console again, realized her fiery and treasonous look was aimed at the GPS. That morning, he didn't understand why she required navigational guidance from an airport she'd driven to for forty years. "Road construction," she explained, though he couldn't find a single work sign, highway cone, or hardhat.

"She sounds sexy," he had teased her. *"For a good time, make a right at the light."*

"Leave her alone," she had said.

"These GPSs can be such vamps, guiding the trusting against traffic on one-way streets, or smack into the middle of lakes."

"Not mine." Her undeniable faith unsettled him, evoked a prick of jealousy.

The disembodied voice accompanied them on silent errands to Costco and the drugstore, both within two miles of her home, a split ranch where he had grown up. The GPS was no help in the parking garage, however. There were basic, elemental tasks technology expected the human brain to handle alone.

They descended to the fourth level but missed the next exit ramp.

"Let me have the wheel," he said. "Dad's heart surgery took less time."

She slammed the brakes. Tires screeched in the torturous emptiness.

"I know what you're thinking," she said. "Should something happen to him, I won't be able to function. Your dad is the one with the sense of direction. He does all the driving."

Tears fell and she slapped at them as if they were ravenous insects.

"I was thinking about getting home and taking a long piss," he said. But he was shocked by his father's condition after surgery, unprepared for the bloodless pallor, the booby-trapping wires and tubes and urgent alarms, his choking helplessness.

"If we can't find our way out of a parking garage, what are his chances of leaving the ICU?" he said.

"Get some sleep?" she sighed. "I'm expected to go home and close my eyes?"

They stared ahead to the smoky borders of the headlights. The hot air blowing from the heater couldn't touch his chill. His father might die. He wasn't ready to live his life with only memories of him. Like laughter, the shivering got worse the more he tried to repress it. His family and home were far away. His kids, when they grow up, will probably flee him and his wife and come back east, and he wouldn't blame them. When you're young, life's frustrations play out as a multiple-choice exam whose easy answer, though not always the correct one, is distance.

She wiped her nose on her jacket sleeve. "Did I tell you how I got this coat, this warm coat? It was a return, so the price was slashed 50 percent. I talked them into giving me the 30 percent off store sale, too. *And* I had a store credit. This coat cost me $4.13."

"That's great, Ma."

"Four dollars and thirteen cents for essentially a new winter coat that originally sold for a hundred fifty."

She gripped the wheel stiffly, as if the car might buck and throw them. She was retired, her career formidable and rich with accolades. And yet, to defend her abilities, she chose a sale successfully bargained to the hilt.

She reached over and found his hand. Her fingers were still wet with tears.

"Do you want my coat? You can use it as a blanket."

"Let's get going," he said, squeezing her hand, wondering when it became so small and frail. The car seemed too big for her, the parking garage a cruel maze.

"In twenty feet, make a left at the down-facing arrow."

He tried to sound serious, devoid of all mockery.

She hummed to herself, pretending not to listen.

"At the bottom of the ramp turn left."

The tire treads screamed as she cut bold turns down to street level.

"Pay the morbidly obese man in the booth," he said, and waited for the real GPS to locate them.

2

Emotional Contagion

Jimmy has tired red eyes that droop at the corners when he's really pissed. He appears ready to nap so I'm a little worried. "What's gotten into you?" I say. "Maybe a taste of what I got last round?"

I can't remember whether it was Dr. Ben Accomb or his grad student Susan who injected me last round, only that I became scared of life. My heart punched through my chest and each breath crushed my lungs. I thought I'd vanish like the others into the forever of the Operating Theater. But afterwards, I woke up back in Cage #8, staggered into a hollow morning, which meant more empty cages. Bearing this type of quiet is never easy, but it was torture that time. I didn't know what to feel. Lucky? Luck should never hurt this bad.

"If you want your space, I understand," I hear myself saying to Jimmy. This round, the test drug loves me. I'm hugged inside a warm pocket. This peacefulness feels like a dream when the best we can ever hope for with each new round is tolerable and short-lasting pain.

"Suit yourself," I say. But when I turn to leave, Jimmy whisker-whacks me.

"You don't get it," he says.

"Then talk to me, Jimmy."

He nips my white-furred rump, a bloodless warning bite. It doesn't hurt, but it's enough to pinch a hole in this pocket of love. My body grows heavy as this well of good feeling begins to leak.

"Listen. I'm sorry this round didn't treat you well," I say. "But remember who you are. This isn't an alley behind a one-star Thai restaurant. We're bred special."

"If that's what you need to hear," he says.

"That's not it," I say. "But I'm hopeful."

"Hopeful?" He laughs. "For what?"

"For your sake, I hope this lab is testing a new antidepressant."

Two rats patrol the perimeter of our cage, casting stares that are as vacant as Jimmy's. Perhaps I'm part of the control group and they're the treatment group. Or vice versa. Identifying my group has never been this hard. "We're friends," I say. "Remember that."

The other rats titter. Jimmy kicks corncob bedding with his back legs, sprays them with their own urine. "Not cool," they yell and scurry away.

"What? I wouldn't find out about Louisa?" he says to me.

I wedge into the cage corner. These housing units don't include separate play areas. With no space for retreat, aggressive posturing is more likely to escalate to violence.

"Louisa? That's what this is about?"

The others nod their heads in unified disappointment.

"Susan recorded hypersexual behavior. That's the buzz around Rat Enrichment."

"You believe a blonde grad student with dreadlocks? Who wears tie-dye T-shirts with sayings like, *There's no ME in TEAM, only TEA?*"

Disappointment drips from his body.

"She exaggerates her observations," I say. "Projecting her own relationship issues."

"This isn't funny," says Jimmy, his eyes drooping.

"I'm not laughing," I say, locking into Jimmy's stare. "It was the night before last round, the one that almost did me in. Louisa couldn't sleep." I pause, breathing hurts. "She had that feeling. I felt it, too. Why didn't I end up in the Operating Theater? I don't know. Probably because of who I am."

Jimmy now aims his bites at my side. He's smart, knows that rats instinctively protect the face. But I know what he knows, and block each move. "Someone has forgotten who's the dominant rat." Why did I say that? My strength is more internal, the ability to absorb, endure, and persevere. "I was feeling so damn good this round," I say, shaking off a chill.

I dart to the center of the cage, give the two rats a look that erases their smart-ass grins.

"We shared fame, Jimmy. We made history together."

"What?"

"That study freed us from the truly awful labs, gave us very good lives."

The world saw a video where Jimmy was trapped in a plexiglass tube that I desperately climbed and gnawed at to free him. This wasn't newsworthy, though my response to his distress seemed to make grad students proud, as if confirming a noble quality in themselves. Then researchers tempted me with chocolate chips. Now I faced a dilemma. Rescue the scared-looking Jimmy or hoard the chocolate for myself. But I sprung the cover, freed Jimmy, and shared the chocolate booty. This behavior stunned researchers and showed the world that rats could be altruistic, too.

"Where's this good life you talk about?" says Jimmy.

"You always hated how you looked in that tube."

"Imagine how you'd feel? I'll save you the trouble. It sucks."

"You were stuck and didn't know what I'd do. But if you were in my position? Most rats would be paralyzed, too stressed or anxious to move. I'd still be trapped to this day."

"You are trapped," says Jimmy.

"This is our life. It's who we are. And it's a special job."

"You're crazy," says Jimmy.

"OK. Maybe *fated* is a better word. Science needs us. I believe in fate. It brought Louisa and me together in the energy drink study, the one where they shoved tubes down our throats and dripped in liquid fire. I was delirious from the pain. Louisa nursed me and never left my side. Why? We'd never met before."

"You're making this up."

"Without her, there's no way I'd emerge from the flames. No way. She felt my distress, and a few nights ago, before that awful round, I felt hers. Of course I'm going to comfort her. It's what rats do."

Jimmy lunges at me. I drop down, protect my head. I sense that I'm alone, that nobody is responding to my distress. But I proved that rats are capable of empathy. Maybe it was just me, or maybe—and this idea hurts worse than his bites—these rats empathize with Jimmy?

The florescent lights click on. Susan stands before the shelves of cages, sips her usual morning diet cola. She lifts Jimmy off me and sweeps him up. I wish she would drink coffee. Every lab rat has a horror story of a relative tortured in artificial sweetener studies.

Susan and Dr. Accomb examine my injuries.

"This one appears stunned," says Susan.

"Shock from the assault," Dr. Accomb says.

"Not at all," I scream, a pointless act, as rats speak at frequencies beyond the range of human hearing. "Bruising from disloyalty."

"Screw you," says Jimmy, clawing and squirming in Susan's grasp, yoked in an impossible-to-bite position. This isn't him. It must be the drug. She flips through the black hardbound journal. "These two received the same drug."

"Seriously?" Dr. Accomb says.

"Seriously?" I say.

They're intrigued by Jimmy's behavior, which typically means a visit to the

Operating Theater. Susan carries him to the steel table, wrestles him flat and examines his body. I scratch at the cage walls. Sloppy, I know, drawing attention to myself in this way, especially when he's beyond saving. Dr. Accomb rubs his goatee. "What's up with him?" Dr. Accomb asks Susan.

I stop, look up, convey vulnerability with a tilt of my head. Researchers know of our work together, my history with Jimmy.

Dr. Accomb lifts me by the scruff of the neck and nods his chubby, handsome face. From up close, I can read in his blue, neurotic eyes that he's someone in danger of losing grant support. From this height I can also lob a look at Jimmy, who gives a martyrish sigh, angles up from the bed of the Operating Theater. "I loved her," he declares, as Susan slides the hood over his head.

"Let me talk to him," I yell, but the unheard words, having no safe place to land, just fly away. Susan turns on the gas. Muscles spasm, then surrender into an unnatural stillness. "Jimmy?" I say, dumb with sadness, disturbed by a mindless urge to rescue someone I don't want to help.

·   ·   ·

The Operating Theater is a small room off the lab. Dr. Accomb had dashed out, grumbling how he's late for an evening meeting, and left the door half-open. Our eyesight stinks, but we know the blurred image in the lamplight is Susan taking a scalpel blade to Jimmy's belly.

"That's wrong," says a young rat with 26 written onto the base of his tail, punishing the mirrored, tinkling toy that hangs in the Rat Enrichment cage. "Shoving it in our faces."

"No pensions for lab rats," I say, hopping onto the wheel and creaking it hard. How could Jimmy and I receive the same drug and respond so differently? Exhaustion helps push away thoughts that I don't want to think about. The same drug? I need distance, too, but sprinting faster leaves me exactly where I started.

"If it bothers you, don't look," I say to Rat 26. He can't resist the unobstructed view. None of us can. Or maybe he doesn't hear me, my voice lost in the hubbub as rats fall over plastic balls, squirm through hollow tubes, swing at ropes beaded with brightly colored shapes. Experts believe Rat Enrichment to be a space for play or socialization, but it's where we beat away boredom and the dreadful emotions that come with it.

"This is what we do," says young Rat 26, jostling two rats I don't recognize off a ball. "We go down and show her what it feels like to receive pain."

"That's right," echo the two rats he just bullied. "Real pain."

"Wrong," I say, breathlessly pounding the wheel, my heart racing at three hundred beats a minute. "We don't belong in Rat Enrichment at this hour. She'll wonder how we got out of our cages."

"Look at Jimmy. That's not happening to me," a few voices chime from the fringes of the Rat Enrichment cage, which is quite generous in Dr. Accomb's lab.

"We will all look like Jimmy," I say, perturbed by the lack of professionalism in the younger rats. "It's why we're special. It's only a matter of time before some researcher figures out that rats bred for lab work have also been bred to unhitch cage doors. So think."

"Think?" says Rat 26. "What good is that? Let's do what we do before we're too dead to do anything."

He scrambles up the walls of Rat Enrichment. The others follow. Maybe the drug is messing with their heads. Young rats can be so impulsive. I leap from the wheel while spinning quite fast. The awkward jump makes the wheel shake, then tip over on its flimsy base. Some rats dart for safety. But one rat freezes in place, his back begging to be crushed. "Move," I yell, catching the collapsing structure with my shoulder.

"A little help?" I say, my limbs trembling, straining to push it upright. It's late in the experiment. I've every right to be tired. That's what I tell myself.

The stunned rat snaps to attention and scoots off. Rat 26 is wrestling a few others for food hidden in the center of a hollow ball, blind to how it's designed for temptation, not reward.

"Please," I say, feeling small and old, empty except for despair and regret. Do these rats feel my distress and rush to my aid? Do they recognize what's at stake for all of us if Susan turns our way, the new cage security? The wheel collapses, kicks up a cloud of bedding, booms like the world ending. Which isn't far from the truth.

"You almost got us killed," says Rat 26, startled, his tail feigning swordplay. The others hover close, a few poke their noses into my side. Rats are affected by the emotions of other rats; unfortunately for me, the emotion swirling in the air is rage.

I scavenge their faces, find stone instead of sympathy.

"The older wheels were sturdier."

"Real quality craftsmanship, huh," says Rat 26, "back in the day."

Susan is deaf to what's going on, her concentration lost inside Jimmy, which is sad because he wasn't particularly interesting. I've seen it before. The young researcher huddles in the lab later and later until there's an air mattress rolled into the corner, energy bar wrappers littering the desk, and tears piling up in the wastebasket. This basement lab isn't friendly to cell phones. Late at night, Susan's voice cracks from down the hall. I'm a survivor of too many experiments not to grasp the gist of her conversations. No, I'm not *playing* with rats. Of course I love you.

"I begged for some help," I say, nodding to the hollow ball. "But you were preoccupied. Selfishly so."

This happens late in experiments. Survivors recognize that good fortune is being served in smaller and smaller portions.

"Selfish? Us?" says Rat 26. "With your friend's girl. How could you?"

"Louisa wasn't his girl."

"Says you."

"The love was in his head."

"Well, it was in his head deep," says Rat 26.

"Lab rat love doesn't exist. It can't," I say. That denial, spoken outright, triggers a trapdoor in my gut where I can see, with painful clarity, how much I miss her. "Probably whatever Dr. Accomb gave him," I say. "It was the drug."

"This round messed me up," says one rat. "I thought my foot was a chew toy."

"I got the same drug," I say. "I felt snug, peaceful. No. I felt euphoric."

Maybe the drug this round had little, if anything, to do with the way I felt. Instead, it was the result of being with Louisa, the lingering astonishment of love? The last night with Louisa, I tried to focus her attention on our role in the service of science, the meaning it brings to our lives. "Some of us think differently," were the last words she said, softly licking my side. It tickled so much it hurt. I asked her to stop. What an idiot, to resist something that made me shiver with joy.

"When the girl sleeps on the air mattress, we do what we do," says Rat 26.

"Leave Susan alone," I say. "Dr. Accomb left the door open. Don't blame her. What did you think happened in the Operating Theater? Has anyone ever come back from there?"

"Susan?" says Rat 26, disregarding my question. "When were you promoted to pet?"

They surround me, energized by their group strength. If my life-defining work means anything, I must believe that empathy surrounds me too, that someone will leap to my rescue.

"Careful," I say. "You're violating the Suspension of Dominance Agreement."

This unwritten understanding applies only in Rat Enrichment, a neutral space for wellness that wouldn't produce stress-free rats unless we could exercise and hang out free of status markers like aggressor/intruder/defender.

My legs won't move. This is fear. Not fear of death, but death at the hands of irony. How humiliating, to survive as many experiments as I have only to be mauled by fellow rats. "Jimmy and I go way back. They encouraged friendship bonding, before trapping him in the Plexiglass tube to see what I'd do."

The younger generation is blind to my achievements. The nature of the business doesn't foster much industry memory.

"You shared a moment, an experiment," says Rat 26. "That's all."

"No. They didn't control that. The friendship was real."

"Like Jimmy's love for Louisa?" says Rat 26, tuning to the Operating Theater. He gasps and shields his eyes. The others are looking, too. They're really seeing themselves. Flat on their back, limbs pinned down, belly gutted, insides in disarray.

Rat 26 goes quiet, hangs his head, a surprising gesture of respect. Then he covers his mouth. "I'm going to puke."

"Rat's don't puke. We can't."

His choking spasm is close enough to violent retching that I kick bedding over where a mess would have been.

"Let me ask you all a question," I say. "We can get out of our cages without any problem, but why doesn't anyone escape?"

Rat 26 wipes his mouth and glares.

"Because you're lab rats," I say. "You endure from experiment to experiment, but survive on the outside, where the conditions aren't controlled? Forget it."

"Get him."

I jump inside the collapsed wheel, stupidly seek protection behind the mistake that first put me into trouble. My eyes sweep the top of the cage. Was it always this high? I spin around to Susan. "Look up," I scream, but she's lost in her journal, intensely writing with a bloody pencil. Giving our lives to the experiment doesn't mean the experiment accounts for our lives. Jimmy's behavior can't be weighed, dissected, or identified under a microscope.

She tosses a candy wrapper into the trash, stretches her back, and yawns. When her head twists around and finds us, she screams.

"Everybody run," says Rat 26, but her face rises above the cage, brown eyes bloodshot and burdened, lips trembling. We're returned to our cages. Her grip hurts. I don't resist, don't scratch; cooperation is the best way to distance myself from the others.

.   .   .

Dr. Accomb enters the lab balancing two coffees and the familiar bag stained from freshly baked muffins. He flips the lights, and the air cracks with a flickering brightness.

"What's wrong?" he says, unzipping his golf windbreaker.

The tears have been scrubbed from her cheeks. Susan strangles paper towels from the dispenser and blows her nose. "Found some of them in Rat Enrichment."

"And how in hell did they get there?

She stutters. "I can't say."

"How many?"

"Enough."

Dr. Accomb yanks off his rimless glasses.

"I don't know how it happened," Susan says.

"They didn't just unhitch their catches," he says, scanning three shelves of cages.

"The tops were secure," she says. Tears fill her eyes again. "I've been here all night." She nods to the Operating Theater. Cage #8 is on the lower shelf, so I can feel the panic in Dr. Accomb's pacing.

Susan retreats into her hooded sweatshirt.

"I'm so sorry."

Dr. Accomb grunts, slips into his lab coat, fingers the buttons, then impatiently takes off the white coat and returns it to one of the wire hangers hooked behind the front door. He lacks the style of the superstar researchers. He's partial to pleat-beaten slacks and beige Oxford shirts. The open button at the neck betrays a few dark hairs and a few whiter than mine. When working in the lab, he always sports a lab coat, until now.

"I was planning to include this preliminary data when I resubmitted the grant." He rolls the shirtsleeves to below the elbows as if afraid he'll rip the cuffs on his muscular forearms. "You know what happens to the lab if this grant doesn't get a fundable score?"

This is a smaller lab, but cozy. A fishing pole in the corner leans beside a guitar covered in stickers. Having never seen Dr. Accomb without his eyebrows twisted in dead seriousness, I can't imagine him relaxing with a line in the water, or strumming a chord, without the help of a large syringe filled with love and hugs.

"My work is in jeopardy, too," says Susan. "I'm living off your grant."

He sighs, offers her one of the coffees. She slowly accepts it with both hands. "Thanks."

He fingers through the hard-bound journal. "Which animals did we inject yesterday?"

"Animal? I'll show you animal," Rat 26 jeers. The others join him.

"You'll get yourself killed," I scream.

"We're going to die anyway," says Rat 26.

"Not like this. There's a right way," I scream while straining to appear calm. Dr. Accomb can't mistake what upsets me with what upsets them.

"Who got out?" Dr. Accomb asks, running down the list of rats who received injections the last round. Susan points outs several cages, an accusatory finger finds me.

I tilt my head, offer up my best cute rat pose as Dr. Accomb approaches my cage. But Rat 26 steps up his antics, throws himself against the wall and trashes his water bottle. Dr. Accomb shifts his attention, sharpens his focus. Rat 26 is quickly pinned in an impossible-to-bite position. He doesn't give up. He rallies the others into a frenzy as the hood swallows his head. The border between stillness and lifelessness can be hard to identify, but Rat 26 crosses it.

·   ·   ·

Those of us caught in Rat Enrichment are quarantined into solo cages rigged with video cameras. What are they recording? My naps? My back and forth treks about the cage? The dull expression on my face as I watch Susan scribble in her journal and Dr. Accomb crumple papers at his desk? It's hard not to root for them. They mean well. Only they don't know what they don't know.

The first two days in quarantine, I've eyed the Rat Enrichment device in my cage, a swinging rope ladder with a mirror dangling from the highest rung. Short on the muscle and balance of a younger rat, I'll have trouble reaching the top. The video camera will capture my feeble attempts, when the previous video shows me a hero saving Jimmy.

But Rat Enrichment devices are really birdcage toys and I can't allow myself to be intimidated by a bird toy. My first attempt falls short, tinkles the metal balls hanging from the bottom rung. A mocking reward. Nowadays, mediocrity earns everyone a chocolate chip or a tinkling ball. My hind legs burn, my tail drags, but I keep at it. I take one final leap, stretch out, and cling to the top rung. I look tough for the camera, confident in my success. But when my eyes open, an older, distorted face greets me in what has to be, must be, a horribly broken mirror.

"Look how cute," says Susan, smiling, a fresh look for her, championing my human behavior, before she stops, her face gray, as if suddenly aware that her life might resemble mine.

·   ·   ·

The next day I'm returned to a cage with other rats, though it isn't Cage #8.

Two rats pounce up to me, their whiskers on alert. One tail slices the air with the number 43, the other boasts 48.

"What are you holding?" says Rat 43.

"Beat it," I say. "I wasn't injected today."

I see myself through their eyes. I'm vulnerable, exploitable.

"You were on the outside, right?" says Rat 48.

"None of your business."

"How was it?"

They smack their lips, eyes jumpy. They're skin poppers, young rats who bite into others who are enjoying a good high. I do feel rested and cleaned out. During quarantine I focused on getting out, indifferent to what was happening to my body when nothing was being done to it.

"Now excuse me, as it appears I was returned to the wrong cage."

"So you weren't exactly returned, were you?" says Rat 43, sneering.

I give him a whisker-whack. "You know who you're talking to, right?"

"I know," says Rat 48. "Wait, wait. No hints." Rat 43 laughs as his friend snaps his fingers. "It's on the tip of my brain," says Rat 48. "You're a . . . a . . . a . . . lab rat?"

I study their faces. "You really don't recognize me."

They collapse, choke on their laughter, hug their bellies, roll on their backs.

"What's that?" says Dr. Accomb. His chair screeches against the floor.

Susan races to the cages. "Over here," she says. "Seizure activity."

Seizure activity? I want to laugh.

"They were injected yesterday," Dr. Accomb says.

"You can't be serious," I say.

Susan takes them both to the Operating Theater and slams the door. I take the weight of a long silence.

"Are you sure of the drug they received?" says Dr. Accomb from behind the door.

"Of course," says Susan.

"That one, too?"

"Yes."

"And the others?"

"It's all there, in writing. Timed and dated," she says, punctuated by a metallic thud that I assume is the hard-bound journal striking the desk.

"My daughter does that," says Dr. Accomb. "And she's six." There's a pause, and a cough. "These findings are potentially very interesting."

"You think I don't know that?" says Susan.

"Careful" he says, his tone insisting upon respect while marking an apology.

"You're both idiots," I scream. "Forget the drug. They were just bullies. Now their deaths go down as sacrifices in the name of science."

"Shut up," one rat says from the next cage.

"The next round better start up soon," says another.

"I heard the protocol was changed."

"Who cares, as long as it's not an LD50 gig."

"What's that?" says a younger voice.

"Toxicity trial. Find the dose that kills 50 percent of us. Don't give two shits if the drug works."

"It's undignified," someone chimes.

Their voices bounce from all around my head. Are they the controls from the ADHD lab?

"It's hard, too, on those who survive," I say. "Watching needless suffering, unable to do anything about it."

"Who do you think you are, someone special?"

"I *am* special," I say. "A star in a landmark study. My video shown at conferences all over the world. Magazines covers."

"What about Rat 26?" a low voice says. "They were coming after you before he started acting crazy and got Dr. Accomb's attention. Is he special, or just doing what rats do?"

"What?" I say. My heart's hammering, doing its own clumsy dance. My body tries to resist the urge to tremble along with it. My thinking is shattered by a thunderclap, the unlatching of my cage.

"Look at him. So docile," says Dr. Accomb.

"This one?" she says, pulling me upwards.

Docile? Tenacious maybe, or resilient. Susan will vouch for me. She checks the number on my tail, then shuffles the pages of her journal. "He was quarantined. But look what he got before that," she whispers. I still can't believe Jimmy and I had received the same drug.

Dr. Accomb studies me. "His behavior is different from the others."

Susan examines me upside down, fixed in an impossible-to-bite position. Her hold is tighter than before. I can tell she's tired, not long for this lab. Maybe medical school, or a biology teacher, or a science writer penning articles about altruistic rats, reminding the world that calling someone a rat is really a compliment.

Why should I feel anything for Susan? She disrespected us by dissecting Jimmy in view of the housing area. She doesn't remember me, if she knew me at all.

Soon, the other rats start in again, carousing, kicking food trays. They should learn, but can't help themselves. Then again, if the larger group in an experiment displays crazy behavior, acting quiet and calm can prove perilous and irresponsible. They're cheering me on. They have to respond this way, even if they can't help me, because it eases the distress of watching.

Susan pinches the scruff of my neck upward to immobilize my head. Her hands smell of soap and antibacterial foam, false fragrances straight out of every lab rat's nightmare. I fight back. I hadn't received an injection for days. They'll find nothing, or record a broken heart and a brain waterlogged with disillusionment and think them caused by a chemical belonging to their study design. I twist around, flip Susan the bird. The rats go crazy.

Then, moving toward the Operating Theater, she does the strangest thing. She stokes my back, gently, which I've never seen done with the others. Pets must be held in this manner, caring for caring sake; the poison in that thought is unbearable. My teeth dig into her finger. She curses and begins to cry. I wanted to hurt her, but not cause pain, and that's difficult to reconcile. Dr. Accomb swoops in and I retreat behind my eyes before the hood fits over my head.

"You OK?" says Dr. Accomb.

"I'm good," I say, though my voice is muffled in warm darkness, and the question was meant for Susan.

The air tastes sweet under the hood. I know that altruism isn't a purely human endeavor. Each breath pulls me further from my body. I drift into a space between memory and dreams. I hear the story Louisa told me during our last night together, about her friend who suffered through a new anticoagulant drug experiment. They put him to sleep and a razor made a cut into his tail. Researchers counted the time before a clot formed and bleeding stopped. He awoke in excruciating pain. When the pain eased, they put him out again. He dreamed like crazy but awoke in greater agony with another scabbed slice in his tail. They put him out a third time, and a fourth. By then he'd lost quite a bit of blood. His tail was deformed with mounds of scabs. Hoping to ease the pain, Louisa gently licked his tail, but he screamed *no*. "What can I do? There must be something," she begged. He told her not to worry. He'd seen paradise. Cages without walls, rats floating far above the pain.

3

Soft Landings

"For Sale" signs, the new neighborhood flower, are blooming everywhere this summer. Every morning I run five miles, and every morning I notice another abandoned property. I didn't start mowing these overgrown yards because a twenty-five-year-old with a BA in Liberal Studies dreams of cashing in his B average for a career as a lawn stylist. But my hometown appears to me as a lonely, scrappy kid with lice in his hair, in desperate need of a bath and haircut, who people are content to let stink and scratch.

I already work at a baseball camp, coaching kids to become future major leaguers. Though scouts ignore me, the fire to play pro ball eats at my gut. My mother insists this burning I feel is really an ulcer. But that's mom, a shut-in swallowed up by depression after my father's death six years ago. I still live at home. We get along better once baseball signs replaced my nagging. The bunt signal—tapping my nose—means showering and changing clothes might not be a bad idea. Brushing my chest and going to my belt reminds her to open a can of tuna or down an Ensure shake. My father, an unlucky but eager weekend fisherman, could always light a smile by asking her to picture optimism leaping like salmon through her veins. Once, after a whitewater fishing vacation in Idaho, he had her giggling with a tale of how salmon jumped into his arms and bathed themselves in lemon.

During a game today at the Sampson College baseball camp, I'm reminded how salmon fight the currents to spawn, only to die. I'm waving Spike home on a ball hit sharply up the middle. I'm thrilled for this bony kid. He's dragged his team down the past week, but now he'll cross the plate, tie the game, get pounded with a hero's welcome. But he sputters after rounding third. Halfway home, he stops completely. His teammates leap from the dugout, screaming so hard that when the catcher slaps the tag for the final out I'm afraid they're going to puke. Spike defiantly finds a seat at the end of the dugout. His teammates, their mouths emptied of all words, start flinging their gum at him.

"Cut it out. Don't you know about the gum control laws?" I say, pacing the dugout. This awful joke buys time as I sort through my disappointments. I'm pissed at the gum throwers for sure, but I'm also upset with Spike.

"Mistakes are part of learning," I say, not entirely convinced it was a mistake. "We all make mistakes. Teammates must support each other."

"Why?" a kid yells back at me.

I kick at a few pebbles. "Because we can't play this game alone."

Afterward, Spike's mom slams me for being irresponsible, for pushing him to do something he wasn't ready for. "In my experience, kids love scoring runs," I say.

"But he didn't score, did he?" she says, injecting me with this look of pity that gnaws on my bones, even after I return home that evening. I scrub myself raw in the shower, wearily chanting, "You're an optimistic guy. You're an optimistic guy."

.   .   .

Showered, dressed in jeans and a golf shirt, I hold the bat high, take my stance on the porch, and stare down my reflection in the front door storm glass. The major league pitcher I pretend to be facing throws heat at ninety-five, pops the 60 feet 6 inches from mound to home plate in four-tenths of a second. He'll use my anticipation against me, set me up with slow junk—breaking balls and change-ups—that are never as pretty as they appear. The ball's thirty feet away. I have a quarter of a second to pull the trigger, to believe what I see. "Don't commit too early," I remind myself. "Let the ball travel."

Soft hands and baseball smarts kept me in the starting lineup at second base all four years in college. By now, most guys in my situation—older, medium height, soft body, streaky bat—have the good sense to move on. I'm giving myself until the end of the summer to snag a tryout with a pro organization. Before her mind imploded, my mother would say it takes desire and imagination to recognize one's critical limitations.

.   .   .

A grating horn breaks my focus. What sounds like a wild goose in pain belongs to Thistle's VW bus, a rust-trap bought at a police auction years before. "What's up, Cape?" she says, as if she stops by all the time. She jumps from the VW, slams the door. I lean on the bat, take slow breaths. Dressed in work clothes—long black skirt, white blouse and black heels—she must be the sexiest accountant on the planet. Her dark hair is short, no longer the crazy ponytail down to her lower back. We used to hang out in our asexual years. Since then, we've exchanged waves and hellos, always in passing. Now her wispy body stands at the bottom of my stoop.

"Nothing much. What's up with you?" I say.

"Could I borrow you for an hour?" She appears distressed and embarrassed by it.

I take my batting stance. Her reflection joins me in the glass as she rises up the cracked cement steps. "Depends."

"I need muscle," she says. "Annie's at Trickling Creek Nursing Home. She fell. I need you to keep the nurses away while I take care of her."

She's stroking my ego. Growing up just down the street, she'd seen me pumping weights in my open garage before and after school and never adding bulk to my frame.

"What the hell is Annie doing at the Creek?"

"Cracked hip. The doctors replaced it and sent her to the Creek for rehab. But she's got a touch of dementia. The social workers say she's a fall risk, even if she's living with me."

"I hate the Creek." I focus on turning my hips, rolling the wrists. "Hate it."

My father was a "Creek" resident for eight years before he died. Skull crushed in a construction accident, he emerged from a coma into a world of confusions. "Who was this kid claiming to be my son? Why does this depressed woman forcing pie into my mouth say she's my wife? Why doesn't the staff let me go fishing in the trickling creek?" He'd wander off in search of the creek. Eventually, they anchored him to a chair, leather clasps on his wrists and a mesh vest around his chest. He withered in restraints, but it saved him from learning the truth—a creek didn't exist. What a relief when he died. At the funeral he reclaimed his dignity. People remembered the man, not the patient.

.   .   .

We find Annie on the floor beside her bed. My stomach turns at the blood-stained towel pressed against her short silver hair, pooling with jelly clots.

"Let me guess. You weren't using your walker," says Thistle.

"My bladder was bursting," she says.

Blood drips down Annie's cheek. Thistle digs into her knapsack, orders me to rip open gauze. My hands shake. I can't reconcile the Annie before me with my memories of her gardening for hours with her sleeves rolled up. She had a sweet smile, hooded eyes, a sharp Roman nose, and little patience for chitchat. From behind, she and Thistle could be mistaken for sisters.

"Laceration #3 opened up again. This is #3B," Thistle says to Annie, loud enough for the staff to hear. Thistle has cataloged each laceration zigzagging across Annie's face and scalp since she entered Trickling Creek a month before. Thistle bandages madly, ignores requests from people dressed in scrubs to step aside. Tense moments pass before they push her away, unroll Thistle's work and start over.

I feel waves of heat beating off Thistle's body.

Annie's eyes dart to me. I avoid her gaze, afraid she can read my animal fear of ever becoming as dependent as she is.

"Who are you?"

"Cape," Thistle says. "From down the street."

"Cape?" She pauses as if her memory of me is tucked away on a high shelf just beyond her fingertips. "The baseball player?"

"Yes, ma'am," I say. Once proud of this association, it now feels fraudulent.

"Why are *you* here?"

I give Thistle a probing look. "That's an excellent question."

.   .   .

We follow the ambulance to the emergency department. The silence drowns out the VW's clanking engine. Thistle and I had traveled in different circles in school—mine included sports geeks who watched ESPN on Friday and Saturday nights drinking beer—dateless experts of women. Thistle worked most nights, either waitressing at Carlati's Pizza Pub or tutoring math. She was mature and preoccupied, mysterious and unattainable. Annie once chased the captain of the basketball team from her porch with a crowbar.

Thistle and I knew more about each other than we cared to admit. Rumors floated above the street. When the rental car agency promoted Thistle's mom to a management position—but in Tucson—along with her supervisor boyfriend, she didn't ask Thistle to join her in the new life. Annie kicked out the mom and changed the locks. We were nine or ten at the time. Mothers didn't leave their kids. Grandmothers weren't like Annie, who left her husband the first time he hit her, and told stories about the many times she was arrested and clubbed protesting Vietnam.

"She'll be alright," I say. "Annie's a fighter."

Thistle's large brown eyes are luminous with hurt.

"I asked you to keep the nurses away from her. Did you do that?"

"They were standing around her when we arrived. They work there."

We stop at a traffic light before the hospital entrance.

"Some are good, and some . . ." She rubs her mouth. "I needed you."

"You asked me to come and I did. I *was* working on my swing."

"Do you really believe you're a prospect at what, twenty-five?"

"I'm trying to stay optimistic," I say, burying my hurt in a long pause. "For ten years we've barely rubbed two sentences together. Now you act as if I've let you down?"

Thistle clutches. The van lurches and screeches into the hospital parking lot. "I need a cigarette."

"You still smoke? I thought it was a prop in high school, a way to give your voice a sexy edge."

Thistle marches into the ER two steps ahead of me.

"I smoked for six years. Quitting wasn't easy," she says, arms crossed. She stops, turns. "It was fucking hard."

Anger flashes off her face, then curiosity and wonder. Opposing pitchers click through these expressions after I've jacked their nastiest pitch out of the yard.

.   .   .

The ER nurses know Annie, greet her affectionately. They smile stiffly at Thistle. "She needs sutures, not staples," Thistle tells the doctor. "A two-layer closure."

Bruises ring Annie's eyes; scars run about her face.

"You can go," Thistle says to me, her arms folded as if fighting a chill.

"Let Cape stay," says Annie, her face now covered by a sterile drape. "Unless you have some place you need to be."

"Not really," I say.

"That's sad," says Annie. "You're too young to have nothing to do."

I don't tell Annie about the baseball league I play in three nights a week. Or how this past spring, I struck deals with realtors and banks to tend to the wild lawns on unsellable and foreclosed properties, those where weather-beaten "For Sale" signs had *For Ever* spray-painted at the bottom, or *For Saken* or *ForePlay to Decay*. If I find out who did this, I'll kick his ass. Negativity doesn't push people to buy houses.

"Say Cape," asks Annie. "Is your mom still making those incredible apple pies?"

"Not so much."

"Nobody makes pies anymore," she says. "Why's that?"

The doctor stops suturing, raises her head thoughtfully.

"Maybe people don't *eat* much pie anymore," says the doctor.

"Too bad," says Annie, "I wouldn't fall down as much if people ate pie."

I'm puzzled. The doctor tilts her head. Thistle sighs. Was this cryptic wisdom, a nut worth cracking, or thoughts from a tired mind we should respectfully let float away?

"Why did she stop baking pies?" Annie says.

"Arthritis in her hands," I lie. "She'd roll her own dough. It hurt too much." I don't talk about my mother's depression, her love for a man lost to us. She stopped baking pies, my father's favorite dessert, because he chewed with a tight, pleasing expression, as if he knew he should be enjoying it more than he was.

·   ·   ·

The next day at baseball camp, I find Spike. "Why did you stop?" I ask. "All you had to do was run home. Run a straight line. Move those legs."

"I didn't feel like it," he says. He's handsome with sandy blonde hair and a distracted quietness seen in geniuses and sociopaths.

"C'mon," I say, chuckling. "Rarely is success in life such an easy dash. Rarely does it require more effort to fail."

Fail. People dance around the word nowadays, but I boldly say it. Spike looks around, as if bored with me. "Can I go to the bathroom, Coach?"

·   ·   ·

Is Spike messing with me? That question laps back and forth in my mind while I battle a new lawn that evening. Damp, knee-high grass glops the mower blade, repeatedly killing the engine. A one-hour job takes two, and finishing the job requires a headlamp and extra mosquito spray. But I find calm in the brainless act of mowing lawns, the vibrating engine, the orderly wheel tracks as the mower cuts through grass and crab grass, dirt and dog shit, kid's plastic shovels and water-logged baseballs, and, lately, crack vials and broken beer bottles.

Even the most devastated yards appear prouder when I'm done with them. My pulse races, my lungs burn, my spine straightens. It's easy to misuse this confidence, believe similar work and effort will bring me a shot at pro ball. I dream cautiously.

The tires of Thistle's VW scrape the curb. Brick red fingernails flick cigarette ash out the window.

"Annie fell again," she says, without even a hello. "Laceration #4."

I wipe sweat from my face with the tail of my shirt. "Is she OK?"

"She asked if you'd come. She mentioned that pathetic Batman costume you wore every year for Halloween when we were kids. Maybe she thinks you can save her."

I'd knock on Thistle's door each Halloween, sweating in the cool autumn. Her smile tasted better than any Hershey's bar.

"You gave me a lot of shit for that costume."

"How could I know the nickname Cape would stick?"

I push the mower away, sulking like a kid. "Send her my best."

"You're not coming? She's asking."

"What about you?"

Thistle shrugs, drags on a cigarette. "I started smoking again," she says. "Stress."

I swat at mosquitoes diving around my head. The air feels heavy and electric and smells the way summers used to smell. Charcoal clouds hold an evening shower. A long-forgotten memory from high school cracks like lightning.

"We were in high school," I say to Thistle. "Annie was out for her morning walk. She found me passed out on my lawn. I was hung over, without a clue how I got there. She pulled me up, picked grass off my face, and took me back to your house. She called my mom—who thought I was still asleep—and covered for me, saying she had become woozy while out for her morning walk, that *I* had helped *her* home."

.   .   .

"Number four, definitely #4," says Thistle, stomping outside Annie's room.

"Even if we move her closer to the nurse's station," says the nurse, "that doesn't mean we can watch her all the time. We have many residents to care for."

"So you let her walk around and fall and crack open her skull?"

"She knows she's supposed to use her walker. She chooses not to."

"She has dementia," I say, in the impatient tone used on the kids when they let the ball scoot between their legs. The nurses eye me suspiciously. Thistle fires me an expression of pained surprise.

Dr. Gupta emerges from the room pleased with himself. "The wound closed nicely with steri-strips. A visit to the ER will be unnecessary."

"Until it opens up again," says Thistle, wheeling around to face him.

"Hopefully that will not happen," he says politely.

Thistle rolls her eyes as if they weigh ten pounds.

"What should we do, Miss? We can't tie her down. People are not animals."

"I'm not saying that," says Thistle.

"What is it then?"

Thistle fists the sides of her scalp. "She deserves . . . better."

Dr. Gupta has a slight paunch, intelligent eyes, thick black hair combed in a side part. He takes Thistle's hands in both of his. "We can't give her a life she finds acceptable without risk. Our hands are tied, too."

Thistle keeps shaking her head.

"We will help you consider arrangements to a different home if that is your wish," says Dr. Gupta. Thistle squeezes her eyes tight, as if shutting out the painful reality that I suspect undid my mother. People don't choose the Creek if they have the right health insurance, or enough money. It is the best option for those without options.

Annie appears in the doorway, gauze taped above her left eye.

"What's going on out here?" she asks.

"Why can't you use your walker?" says Thistle. "Is it some kind of protest?"

Annie seems oblivious to the scolding. "Cape, could you find me some OJ?"

"Sure, Annie," I say, and head down a corridor. The smell of urine and over-cooked green beans steaming from food trays pull me into the past. I see my father tied down and pumped with sedatives, sitting in his own piss or shit. My mother crying at the pressure sores tunneling under the skin of his back. Oh, I hated coming here. My mother did, too, but she never admitted it outright. "This is part of love, too," she'd say. Trickling Creek appears nicer now, but the seascape watercolors dressing the walls are so bush-league you can't help but question everything else.

.   .   .

On the way home from the Creek, I suggest that the paintings belong in a cataract museum, where viewers aren't expected to have good vision.

"The frames aren't so bad," Thistle says. "Right?"

"They are what you need them to be." I drop those words out the open window. My head is messed up with memories of my father. For the first time in years I miss him.

"How about the best homemade pasta on the planet?" Thistle says hesitantly, testing my reaction to her offer, or uneasy with the idea that the best of anything might be within our grasp.

"Do you see that?" I say, angrily pointing to three "For Sale" signs with new work by the graffiti bandit. *For Shadow. For Ensic. Fore Skin.*

"It makes this ugliness bearable, don't you think?" she says.

"The wit is trying too hard. It's insulting. It makes things worse," I say.

She moves to speak, then holds her breath. She pulls the VW in front of Ricardo's Place, a client of hers. It's a storefront restaurant in a pulseless downtown strip, rare light behind plum-colored curtains. "Let's eat," she says. "Can we agree on eating?"

Ricardo grabs her shoulders, plants kisses on both cheeks. He politely sizes me up, unimpressed with my T-shirt, the dried sweat, and grass stains. I try to sniff myself without appearing to be sniffing myself as Ricardo, leaning on the backs of empty chairs for support, shows us to a table.

"No menus," Thistle says, as if reading what I was thinking. A loaf of crusty bread appears, along with a carafe of red wine.

"I knew about your dad," she says, dipping bread into olive oil, which I had never seen done before, and motions for me to do the same. "I'm sorry I never said anything."

Olive oil soaks the bread, softens the crust. These tastes and textures are fresh and complicated. Working through them, the crust cutting into my gums, the bread almost sweet, I'm surprised to discover forgiveness. "It was a long time ago," I say. "It's done."

"I can't tell who the good guys are." She sips her wine, sighs. "I think Annie's not using her walker on purpose."

"Screw that. Why would she want to take all these headers? Attention?"

"She was tough with me. The world didn't make sense, she said. I had to be prepared for that." Thistle shrugs. "*She* doesn't make sense."

"Why don't you take her home?" I say. "I'll pitch in. Fuck the Creek."

Thistle pulls out a pile of flat, rubbery sunflowers from her knapsack. "Annie gave me these cuttings as a present. From her garden, she said." I hear the ache when Thistle laughs. "She took scissors to the shower curtain in her bathroom."

I take the small bouquet, inhale the toxic aroma of plastic, bleach, and mildew.

Seriousness wrinkles the corners of her eyes when she looks at me. "You had an eye on me in high school. Why?"

I place the sunflowers on the table. "Why did you ask me to the Creek?"

Bowls of steaming pasta with clam sauce are set before us. She pushes hers away, grabs my hand. "Of the old group on the street, we're the only folks left," she says.

My throat tightens. She's not teasing. "So I'm the last guy on the desert island?"

"This is a desert island?" She fingers the breadbasket. "I saw you swinging your bat on the porch, still at it. 'How sad and comforting,' I thought."

"Sad?"

"And comforting," she quickly adds.

·   ·   ·

The last day of camp I pull Spike aside. "Why did you stop? Why didn't you want to score?"

"Leave me alone," he screams. His father witnesses the tantrum and casually approaches. I expect anything from a lecture to a fist across my jaw.

"Does Spike like baseball?" I ask.

"Loves it," his father says, offering an apologetic grin. "He just doesn't get it."

·   ·   ·

The next two weeks, Annie falls and opens up lacerations #5 and #5A. After laceration #6, which includes #5B, Thistle confronts Dr. Gupta, freezes him with a look of reckless and lethal contempt. He stands before her, his back straight, his eyes lowered.

"Does this ever end?" she asks. Her arms hang lifelessly. We know the answer but need to hear it spoken aloud to keep everyone accountable.

"It's OK," says Annie, taking Thistle by the shoulders. Suture tracks curl and intersect madly about her face and scalp—a map of chaos, or endless misdirection.

"Don't you hate the stink of this place?" Thistle asks Annie, asks everyone.

"It's not a flower shop," I say. Over the past few weeks, I've sensed that I'm perceived as the reasonable one. "It smells of people doing their best."

.   .   .

I hire two kids to help mow lawns. The bank alerts me that more work is coming and offers me a business loan. "Mowing lawns isn't a business," I say to Rivers, the bank's loan officer, aggravated by success I never wanted. "It pays the bills. I'm a baseball player." I played college ball against Rivers. He shakes his head, pushes across his desk a thick loan application. His expression mimics that of the Creek's nurses whenever they *offered* my father a paper cup filled with sedatives.

The calluses on my hands, once evidence of my dedication in the batting cage, now remind me of years of practice without success. I visit my old college coach. He picks at his chin as he studies me in the batting cage. "Not bad, Cape," he says, pondering the chew he spit in the dirt. "You've got the skills of someone who'll make a solid coach."

The sun burns through my neck to my spine. I feel liquid and weak.

"I might have an opening. Shitty pay but long hours."

"I'm a player, not a coach," I say. I describe my Spike problem.

He spits into the dirt again. "Jeez, Cape. He's fucking eight years old."

.   .   .

A day later, I'm sneaking a lead off second base, pride still bruised. My passion and talent now feel like cheap goods, shadows that only appear real against the background of an unimpressive life. I consider my visit to the Creek that afternoon, Annie scuffling with her walker down the corridor, back hunched, face twisted with disdain.

"That's it, Annie," Thistle cheered. "Feel the floor. The floor is your friend."

My mind snaps into the game. I take off on a single ripped into right field. The third base coach motions for me to brake at third. I slow but don't stop.

Annie's walker creaked. The rubber feet squeaked. How could anyone with any pride be faulted for not wanting to be dependent on something that creaks and squeaks?

For the first time in my life I blow through a coach's sign. I kick into gear, charge toward home. The catcher guards the plate, punches his mitt. My legs feel like cement blocks. My cleats sink into the base path. Home plate seems so far away, tucked into a dazzling sunset that for the first time feels intended for someone else. The catcher hugs the ball, lowers his center of gravity, blocks the plate. He must see my desperation, smell my need for a collision. But I don't want to hurt him. That last thought rings through the pain when I regain consciousness and the sun, bright as a knife, stabs me in the eyes.

. . .

"I don't have enough reasons to come to the ER?" says Thistle when she finds me strapped to a backboard.

"The doctor says this crap is necessary until they know my neck isn't broken."

"Are you OK?"

"Hell no. I was called out."

"One of your coaches said you were supposed to hold at third."

"I didn't want to stop. If driving I might have run a red light."

Thistle pulls back her hair. "You told him to call me?"

"I don't remember." My neck is locked in a rigid collar, otherwise I'd turn away.

Her lips twist. She might hold my hand. Instead, she nags a nurse for an ice-pack on my head. "I'll be back," she says, grabbing her knapsack. "I need a smoke."

She leaves and takes the air with her. "Hello?" I call out. I'm tied down flat on my back, helpless. My eyes play tricks. The ceiling stained with drops of blood looks like a floor pocked with holes. I've lost guideposts, can't decide whether I'm falling or flying. "Hey!" I yell, struggling to sit up. The nurses chew me out. I risk possible paralysis if I have a neck fracture. Did I want that? Shit no. But I unsnap the buckles trapping me to the board. I tear the collar from my neck. Hands push me down. Sedatives fuzz my brain. Words fly away from me. "Get him to CT to rule out a head bleed," a doctor says.

. . .

I didn't want to be paralyzed. I didn't want to be difficult. I wanted a mysterious third option. One that wasn't offered and I couldn't describe, but one I'd recognize once I saw it. Doctors say I suffered a concussion. Thinking still hurts two days later. I'm wearing my skin inside out. I feel cut open. I'm scared as a kid is scared—my limbs icy and bloodless—like the time I threw a Nerf football over my brother's hands. It struck a South American ceramic bowl coveted by my mother. The bowl slid a few inches, but remained atop the end table, bowed but undamaged. Nerf allowed us to play ball indoors.

.   .   .

"You're giving Annie the green light to fall," Thistle says when I track her down outside the Creek, smoking.

"She's going down. Accept that," I say. "No walker plus no restraints equals fall."

"Maybe you did damage your brain. You've become just like them. You care with cruelty."

"No. We'll cover the floor and all hard surfaces with Nerf. A Nerf ball bounces off a lamp, the lamp remains unbroken."

"Annie falls and pops back up," Thistle says, mocking my enthusiasm. "Right?" She cocks her head, studies me heartlessly. My mom is crazy, and maybe this apple didn't fall far from the tree? "You're not kidding, are you?"

The next two days I shower her with Nerf gifts. She takes the baseball, football, and basketball and pelts me with them, her face on fire. "I thought I could count on you."

.   .   .

The nursing home refuses to Nerfitize her room. Despite severe penalties and taxes and doubts, Thistle drains her retirement account and funds it herself. "Something has to be done for Annie," she says. "Gupta's talk is killing her."

Dr. Gupta says at Annie's age, there's no such thing as a soft landing.

Annie researches the web and finds chemists in Rochester who developed their own foam/rubber mixture. In a week I'm busy covering the floor of Annie's room with a cushiony orange-yellow material that is firm enough to walk on. Soon, Annie is walking, falling, and pushing herself upright. Her room has the bright colors of a child's recreation room, the sweet chemical smell of new toys. The desk, the chairs, the small table, the bed-frame have puffed rounded edges. The room looks otherworldly, like the set of a low-budget sci-fi movie, a fake planet where, for the first time, my deeds match my desires.

.   .   .

A month goes by, no new injuries to Annie. No EMS transports or hospital visits. Her swollen face heals. Deep purple bruises turn green and yellow like the leaves outside and then fade away.

"She's beginning to look like herself again," says Thistle. I smile sadly. Annie hasn't been restored to the woman I remember. Without the shockingly impressive wounds, she seems older now than ever before.

"I'm still scared of falling," Annie says, touching my arm. "Maybe you can invent something so I won't fall?"

"It's called a walker," Thistle interrupts.

.   .   .

Sitting with Thistle on my stoop one night, drinking beer, her arm occasionally brushing mine, I wonder how I find myself in opportunities built on the misfortune of others. But the growing silence, the dark windows up and down the street, the memories of what this place once was, feel like questions I'm expected to answer.

During my next visit, Annie approaches me. "It's gone," she whispers with warrior-like intensity. "The fear's gone."

Annie stretches to kiss my cheek. "Look out for Thistle." She studies me through a distant, charitable haze. Did I look at Spike this way? I don't believe I did.

.   .   .

I accept the bank's loan but also decide to give myself another year to earn a tryout with the pros. I need that possibility, as unrealistic as it may be. Without this particular slant of light, I'm like everybody else groping through the days.

Thistle's VW pulls up to my house the next day. She slams the door. She's crying.

"What's the matter?" I say.

"Annie is unconscious," she says, shaking.

"Not from a fall?" I say.

Thistle nods, throws me the keys. "I'm a mess, a complete mess."

We rush to the Creek. The medics have already left. Dr. Gupta detours to speak with us from behind the nurses' desk. "I'm sorry."

"What happened?" says Thistle.

"She ventured out of her room to the non-foam world. Very unfortunate."

"*What happened?*" says Thistle, trembling behind clenched teeth.

"Maybe she lost her protective reflexes." Dr. Gupta is dressed September casual, beige turtleneck and brown sport jacket. "The neurosurgeon called. Annie has a large bleed in her brain. Her prognosis is extremely poor. You should know that." Dr. Gupta tenses as Thistle turns to leave.

I'm speechless. I desperately wish I had the words to meet a moment such as this.

"The foam wasn't a good idea," I say to Dr. Gupta when we're alone.

"It's visionary," he whispers to me. "The nursing home director wants to Nerfitize an entire ward. He operates many nursing homes. Golden Peaks, Violet Towers, Fern Grotto. You should agree to work with us as a consultant on the first Nerfing Home."

"You can't call it Nerfing Home. It's not Nerf," I say. Dr. Gupta's grin brushes off this detail. Isn't Trickling Creek a nursing home without a creek? Besides, didn't Gupta just say my idea is *visionary?* My heart feels like a tightly rotating curveball well wide of the strike zone and I'm convincing myself that it caught the outside corner.

I find Thistle outside, pacing with a cigarette in her mouth, ferociously alone. "Let's get to the hospital," I say.

She tosses the cigarette, snubs it with the toe of her running shoe.

I pull the VW out of the parking lot and down the narrow drive. Thistle rummages through her knapsack. "Stop the car." At the entrance there's a large wooden sign, *Trickling Creek Nursing Home,* in fancy script lettering. She jumps out, rattles the spray can, and writes *Tricky Croak.* She calmly climbs back in.

"You're the graffiti vandal?" I ask.

She stares straight ahead, unblinking. "Annie started it. She said we needed to fight back."

"You have no right," I say.

"It feels good," she says, offering me the can. "You should try it."

"Destruction of property shouldn't feel good. It's vandalism."

"It's a fucking sign, a piece of wood, that's all." She throws the spray can out the window. "You happy?"

"I'm sorry," I say, unable to locate everything I'm sorry about.

Thistle coughs to fill the cracks in her voice. "She's been happy the past five weeks," she says. "She can't die now."

"She won't," I say.

Her wrist catches a tear diving down her cheek. Thistle pulls my hand to her lap, holds it tightly with both of hers. "You believe that?" she says.

"I do." Our fingers stumble together. My optimism never hurt this bad. "Definitely." I work the clutch, her hand in mine. The VW grinds into first gear.

4

Sunday Night

An imposing four-foot eleven in running shoes and carrot-colored hair, Mrs. Sheila Goldstein clutched her belly and waddled up to the Emergency Department triage desk, where Anna was waiting, stretching her calves and hamstrings. "I'm dying," Mrs. Goldstein cried, her voice bruised by forty years of smoking and from bossing her husband Albert, who she claims died during sleep because he was too lazy to wake up.

Anna checked her sports watch. "You're late this week."

"The pain's ten out of ten." Mrs. Goldstein doubled over. "No, twelve."

"I can only imagine."

"You're too young to imagine this. You wouldn't know where to begin."

Anna grinned. "I'll get Dr. Bullock. He'll want to know that you're here."

But Anna didn't move. Her focus remained locked on Mrs. Goldstein's powder blue dress with white lilies, the snowflake sweater too small to be buttoned, her cherry-red lipstick. Mrs. Goldstein's moaning echoed in the waiting room, which was typically empty whenever the Bills played. Then she made her move, a leisurely swoon, choreographed to allow the athletic Anna to swing around the desk and safely catch her.

Anna lowered Mrs. Goldstein into a chair, placed a cool towel on her forehead, and smiled that smile which belonged to a recent nursing school grad still fascinated by this game they played week after week. She phoned Dr. Bullock in exam room three.

"He's occupied with a finger laceration, Mrs. Goldstein."

"I'm dying and he's busy with a finger boo-boo?"

"Dr. Bullock apologizes and asks if you'll die a little slower," said Anna, encouragingly. "He wants to finish with this patient so he could spend more time with you."

Her penciled eyebrows crossed like swords. Mrs. Goldstein rocked her hefty, hipless body, shaped not unlike the pot roasts she boiled with potatoes Sundays when Albert was alive. This routine continued, only now she spent the evening in the ED for the constipation and loneliness that accrues from eating leftover pot roast day after day.

.   .   .

The thumb laceration didn't impress Dr. Bullock. "Let's clean it up and dress it. It'll close fine on its own," he told Heather Sands, a coed from Interstate Fashion College, whose concrete campus shared a parking lot with Honest Joe's Bargain Plaza. She lowered her gaze, snorted back tears. "A thin scar, what's the big deal," he said.

"I want to be a hand model," she said, burping up Pina Coladas. "My dreams kibashed by a can of cat food. Really? I'm not even a cat person. I was cat-sitting for my neighbor."

Pretending to reexamine the cut, Dr. Bullock studied her long, lithe fingers and soft, alabaster skin. Regal and elegant, they appeared out of place on a body that just missed being pretty: a tiny but blunt nose, a bright big-toothed smile.

She pulled from her purse a postcard of a sculpture of two hands barely touching. "A friend sent me this from the Rodin Museum," she said. "I see your perfect hands!" was printed boldly on back. Dr. Bullock pressed his thumb where the ink ran. The romantic mist of Paris, he thought, trying to resist the memory of strolling with Natalie dreamily along the Seine on their honeymoon.

"Perfect no more," Heather said. Wistfulness dulled her lovely green eyes, a fateful look he knew too well. It exerted itself as his private practice achieved new levels of failure, his aspirations down-shifting to vague and bitter appeals for recovery. But to witness this defeat in someone so young, blind to her own spacious and generous future, was bone breaking.

When the first stitch pierced skin, he instantly questioned his judgment. The sutures might aggravate matters, leave pinpoint scars that will balloon under a zoom lens.

.   .   .

Mrs. Goldstein expected the laxative magnesium citrate and the narcotic pain-killer Dilaudid within fifteen minutes of hitting the door. If not, she reported in the patient satisfaction survey how he was content to let a seventy-two-year-old woman suffer in pain. He had ordered blood tests and CT scans of her abdomen the first few times he evaluated her, but each workup showed nothing except constipation. He tried explaining how Dilaudid effectively treated pain but didn't address the cause of the pain; how a nasty side effect of narcotics was constipation. Each time she hurt him with the survey. *Dr. Bullock doesn't listen. His hands are cold. His eyes bloodshot. He needs breath mints. He must iron his shirts. Does he own a comb?* Most patients tossed the surveys in the trash. Mrs. Goldstein was a retired school librarian with time to burn. *Never again will I return to the ER.* Every Sunday evening, 8 P.M., there she was.

.   .   .

"I'm overdue, I'm overdue. Ohh," Mrs. Goldstein screamed from exam room ten, scorching the dated posters in the back hallway that cautioned against syphilis and hypertension, the great masquerader and the silent killer.

"That woman sounds pretty bad," said Heather, her acne-inflamed cheeks radiating heat. "What decent doctor could ignore such shrieks?" he imagined her thinking.

"She's not as sick as she sounds," he said, concentrating on squaring his knots.

"I'll be dead in six minutes, Bullock," Mrs. Goldstein cried.

Dr. Cummings, the ED Director, had lectured him about Mrs. Goldstein's evaluations. The hospital administrators were not pleased either. If she requested narcotics, make the customer happy. Dr. Bullock swallowed but couldn't fully digest this edict. He trained here in family practice twenty years ago, when it was the old Mercy Hospital. Battling creditors and lawyers in the six months since closing his practice, he's dependent on this steady paycheck, grateful to be working 7 P.M. to 7 A.M., four nights a week. The two other hospitals in the area had already shut their doors.

"You're not sewing a thumb," yelled Mrs. Goldstein. "You're avoiding me."

Sweat milked from his graying neck hairs, chilled his spine.

"Go see her," urged Heather. "It's OK."

"How badly do you want to be a hand model?" said Dr. Bullock, his hand trembling as he drove another stitch. "Because it takes time to do this right."

He raised his head. Her quivering lip a reminder of his former office manager. She'd drummed his head with the numbers. He must work more quickly, see more patients, if the practice was to survive. "I will not let other people tell me how much time to spend with my patients," he fired back. The words landed like a slap to her face. Since that day, regret and sadness settled over his brain, a thick fog through which he now had to navigate Heather's flinching and Mrs. Goldstein screaming, this moment constructed out of misfiring parts.

"Talk to me. What does it take to become a top notch hand model?" he asked.

"I'm only six credits short of my degree in Merchandise Demonstration."

"Terrific," he said, indifferently. "Then what?"

"Off to NYC. A friend's uncle has a friend at the Shopping Network."

One suture left. He steadied his hand.

"I'll be dead in four minutes," crowed Mrs. Goldstein.

Anna poked her head behind the curtain. Dr. Bullock expected to see frustration, stern-faced rage, but she rolled her eyes affectionately. "Do you need anything?" she asked. Night shifts required an older, battled-tested nurse. Wary, even frightened at first, Dr. Bullock accepted Anna's inexperience because it came with fresh eyes, a blue-gray clearer than river water, and a soft heart. Her blonde ponytail bounced from one shoulder to the other when she walked. If not old and bankrupt in many ways, if he could afford one more passion, he'd forgive himself the fantasy of falling in love with her.

.   .   .

"Beautiful job, Dr. Bullock," said Anna, dressing the thumb in gauze.

"The wound closed well," he reassured Heather. But it could've been better. If only Mrs. Goldstein wasn't knocking inside his head. Fortunately, the body healed itself most of the time, wrote its own story. When it's young, anyway.

"That's it," yelled Mrs. Goldstein. "I've died. I'm dead."

"I must go," Dr. Bullock said to Heather.

Heather nodded. "You're the first person I didn't know who treated me like I have a special talent."

"No problem." He recalled those hands of Rodin. They're two right hands. If part of the same body, their beauty signified severe, unseen aberrancy. "Good luck," he said.

"People in the 'business' get perks galore," piped Heather. Once sutured, she appeared intoxicated by her possibilities. "What do you need?" she asked Dr. Bullock. "Lawn furniture? Pool supplies? A Weedwacker?"

He now lived in a two-bedroom apartment with a great view of the twenty-four-hour U-Shop. He possessed no pool and no lawn, only a deck/fire escape big enough for two folding chairs and a snack table. Each month he wrote an alimony check to Natalie. "I'm not leaving because a top medical student was too idealistic for the real world," she said, ten months before. "But over the last twenty-four years, you've become hateful about it."

"I'm still dead," Mrs. Goldstein announced. "It's not fun."

"What would I need?" he asked himself. If he didn't leap to Mrs. Goldstein's side, he'd need a new job, maybe a new career. He might need that Weedwacker after all.

He couldn't enter Mrs. Goldstein's room. Not yet, anyway. He visited the bathroom, emptied his bladder, splashed his face. For an instant, the mirror revealed the face of a fatigued, eager intern at the old Mercy Hospital, dragging his bones to the ER in the middle of the night for another admission. Before meeting a new patient, he'd wash in this same bathroom, scrub the dead cells off his face, and always find a layer underneath prepared to smile. The bulb above the sink popped. Dr. Bullock stood alone in the dark, fumbling between past and future for the door with a broken lock.

.   .   .

"You're eating?" he said, entering Mrs. Goldstein's room. Her clothes were folded upon a chair. She lay on the stretcher, potato chips crumbing the chest of her gown.

She spit between her clenched teeth when he examined her. Her muscles remained soft, however. Her doughy skin didn't resist his deep probing.

"I prescribed stool softeners," said Dr. Bullock. "Did you take them?"

Mrs. Goldstein slapped the air with the back of her hand.

"I need my drink and Dilaudid."

"You need fruit and fiber," said Dr. Bullock, "and stool softeners."

She flattened the empty bag of potato chips, folded it into quarters. He brought over a garbage bin. "The pain is asking too much of me," she said. "*Yes?*"

Dr. Bullock winced as her *Yes?* jabbed under his ribs, her playful blackmail week after week. He stepped back, rubbed his face. He was a good doctor once, thorough to the point of self-destruction. "Let's try a rectal exam."

"What? You never did *that* before." She moved uneasily on the stretcher. "I'd prefer Dilaudid."

"This is better. If you're really stuffed up, a little agitation might be in order." He snapped on gloves, then a pair on top of that.

"Is it really necessary?" she said.

Dr. Bullock paused. "We can't have you in here week after week, can we?" He gave himself a moment to reconsider. "It's necessary, now."

He assisted Mrs. Goldstein onto her side. She didn't help as he tugged down her underwear. Rectal exams on women in the ED required a chaperone, only he viewed Mrs. Goldstein as a genderless tormentor. Her buttocks were expansive, pale and veiny. There were bruises, too, paddies of green and yellow swirls. "What's with these bruises?" he asked, cautious about how much concern he wanted to commit to this.

"I slip sometimes," she said, trying not to look back at him. He was hoping for a smooth, uneventful passage for him, something mildly uncomfortable for her. His finger met a hard ball of stool. His face tensed. His search revealed what he didn't want to find. The discovery demanded action he didn't want to do. "Serves you right," he thought to himself. He hooked his finger, began scooping. Mrs. Goldstein screamed.

"Does this hurt?" he said, in a voice that he knew wasn't sympathetic enough.

"Not really."

"Why do you sound like I'm murdering you?"

"What you're doing, it's disgusting."

"Do you think I like this?" he said, trying to speak without breathing, the smell acrid and sweet.

Hips flexed in a fetal position, she anxiously rested her head against her arm as he worked below. "Where is everyone? The place is a morgue."

"Football. The Bills game went into overtime."

"Nobody gets sick during the Bills game?"

"Only during halftime."

Dr. Bullock believed the stool nuggets piling upon the stretcher absolved him from participating in her nervous chatter. What more could she demand from him? His index finger was buried to the hilt. Meanwhile, his mind throttled between focus and distraction, leading him back to Heather's thumb, and an easy and obvious solution that had escaped him earlier. He should've glued the wound. Less time, an equal if not better cosmetic result. Damn it. He kept digging and digging. His finger began to cramp. The body could do such cruel things to itself, he thought. You could trust it only so much.

Anna knocked on the door. "The Bills lost in overtime," she said, panic rising in her voice. "There's a serious line out here."

"It's fine," he reassured Anna. A veteran nurse might complain that the bus just dropped off half the town but would quickly make sense of the chaos. Anna needed his help, but if he left Mrs. Goldstein now, her screaming would incite a riot.

"How about my shot?" said Mrs. Goldstein.

"This is the treatment," he told her. "This will do the trick." The word *trick* sat in his mouth like red wine gone bad that he swallowed anyway. "No shot," he said. "Write what you want on the survey. You're my patient, not my customer. Go find a businessman who would do what I'm doing."

The back of his neck tingled, alert to the patients waiting for him in exam rooms up and down the hallway. "Ooh," she said. "Ooh, my."

Dr. Bullock paused. "What's the matter?" A draft warmed the hairs on the back of his hand, followed by playful, bubbling sounds. "Mrs. Goldstein?"

She wasn't responding. Sheila Goldstein was quiet. Dr. Bullock became very nervous. "Sheila?"

Her colon answered, an explosion that caught his arm and splintered his chest. His rage, so pure and acute, couldn't match the mound on the stretcher, not only the source of their shared agony, but now a totem worthy of reverence.

Anna creaked open the door. "Folks are becoming really angry."

"Handle it," Dr. Bullock barked. "Don't let them control the waiting room."

Anna's jaw dropped. Color left her face. She slammed the door.

"I'm so sorry," said Mrs. Goldstein. Tears filled her eyes. "Put your clothes in a bag. I'll wash them. I'll even iron your shirt."

"Don't worry about it," said Dr. Bullock, wearing Mrs. Goldstein's diarrhea on his chest and arm. He couldn't decide whether this counted as success or evidence that he'd finally hit bottom. Strangely, the answer didn't matter. It couldn't matter. Other patients were waiting for him.

He figured Anna would quit instead of dealing with this fecal tsunami, and he wouldn't blame her. He showered, changed into scrubs. He returned to find Mrs. Goldstein sitting fully dressed on a chair. The room had been scoured. Ammonia cloyed the air. Victory burned in his eyes. Even his tears were confused.

"The stink was so bad, half the people ran out," said Anna, flaring a newly minted world-weary smirk. "They were suddenly cured."

"What am I supposed to do?" Mrs. Goldstein asked.

"Fresh fruit and fiber," said Dr. Bullock. "Stay ahead of the pot roast."

"Next week, what am I supposed to do if I'm feeling better?"

5

Comfortable

"Make him comfortable," said Dr. Sitz, the ICU director, squeezing the bruised arm of the comatose and septic Mr. Jones. He buttoned his white coat with a formality that Lori considered strained and dramatic, then slipped out the glassed-in room.

Comfortable meant morphine, sedatives, and shutting off the ventilator.

Lori finished changing Mr. Jones' dressing, which protected and hid the pressure ulcers, deep caverns into the muscles of his lower back that fit her hand. After making certain his IV was flowing well, she flicked out the air bubbles from the syringe and injected dreamy drugs in lethal doses. After a long minute, synchronizing her breathing with the beat of the second hand on her watch, she turned off the ventilator. The familiar quiet clapped her ears. "He never stays," she said to Mr. Jones, trembling, steadying herself on his now lifeless body.

For weeks she'd been Mr. Jones' nurse, became friendly enough with his wife and daughter to call them Fanny and Crystal. Lori found them in the ICU waiting room, tearful lumps in each other's arms. She froze in the doorway, rubber-banded her wild, dirty blonde curls, wishing time could be wrestled and tied this easily. The first anniversary of her son David's death was only two days away and she felt lost, without clues, about what to do or how to feel.

Lori wanted to kneel before Fanny and Crystal, envelop them in her sympathetic arms. But when they looked up, their glare screamed betrayal. How could she? Hurt balled in her throat. What could she possibly say now? Words were inadequate, even toxic, as potentially dangerous as the bacteria that overwhelmed Mr. Jones and every feasible antibiotic. She ordered up two cups of coffee from the cafeteria, a gesture that felt right and undeniably good. Twenty minutes later, Freckles, the nurse manager, emerged from the waiting room holding the signed papers for disposition of the body, and waving two lipstick-stained Styrofoam cups. Her boyish body confronted Lori. "We can't offer coffee to family members of patients who die in the ICU."

"You're kidding, right?" said Lori, though Freckles wasn't known for her humor. "If we did this for everyone the hospital would go broke."

From the pocket of her scrub shirt, Lori handed over four one-dollar bills. "I've been nursing for eighteen years," she said. "Caring means different things to different people, but when did kindness become a mistake?"

.　　.　　.

The two vehicles crashed at an intersection on a dark, leafy street, at an angle that blurred fault. David's twenty-year-old gangly, ultimate Frisbee–loving body was found splayed in the back seat of his twelve-year-old Honda. The driver of the Cadillac Escalade was an intoxicated county judge, who, privileged to be the sole survivor and witness, claimed David ran a red light. A week later, the judge left the hospital, returned to his wife and three children, and quietly resumed hearing cases. Lori had had little contact with him outside of her nightmares.

That night, as Lori replayed Fanny and Crystal Jones' incriminating opinion of her, the judge called. "Hello?" he said, tentatively explaining who he was.

"You!" Lori's blood froze.

"I'm sorry. I know this must be a shock."

"A shock? No, a shock would feel good," she said and hung up.

She sat up at the side of her bed, head hanging between her knees. The phone rang again. But allowing the answering machine to pick up and record his voice wasn't an option.

She answered but didn't say a word.

"I can't sleep," he said, voice slurred. "It's been a tough year. Hell, I know it was worse for you."

Lori gripped the phone with both hands.

"The boy didn't have to die. Your son *was* drinking and driving, but he didn't have to die."

"His blood alcohol level was .09," Lori said, her voice creaking into outrage.

"DWI is .08," said the judge.

"Other states use .10."

"But he was driving in this state," he said.

Lori grabbed her head, horrified to be in this debate with the killer of her only child. An ED nurse for many years, she counted many police and medics as friends. Those at the crash scene, intimate with the damage and tire marks, agreed the Escalade appeared at fault. The official investigation, however, proved inconclusive.

Lori's best friend Tess nursed on the trauma floor where the judge recovered from three broken ribs. Lori knew the judge's alcohol level had been four times the legal limit, and he wasn't even slapped with DWI. Most people couldn't breathe with so much alcohol bubbling in their blood.

"My son is not a drinker," Lori said, trembling with the slip of the present tense. "He ran college track. He took care of himself. His girlfriend swore he had two beers at dinner."

"Lori," the judge whispered, "our kids do many things we don't know about."

She clenched her fist. David's father, her ex-husband, became an ugly boozer. She and David rarely drank because alcohol had cracked their softest memories into pieces with sharp edges.

"Lori?" the judge said, "Are you there?"

.   .   .

"What were you thinking? He was going to be made comfortable."

Dr. Sitz, Freckles, and other nurses blamed Lori the next morning for saving Mr. Smiley from cardiac arrest.

"It was reflex," Lori said, defending her actions. "The chest thump never works."

For weeks, Mr. Smiley lay dying next door to Mr. Jones. He hadn't left an advanced directive. Two days before, Dr. Sitz revealed the exhaustion of all promise to Mr. Smiley's son Owen.

"If our goal is to get him off the ventilator, off pressors, and off dialysis, we're in trouble," said Dr. Sitz. "I hate the term, but treatment is futile."

"If futile treatment works," said Owen, "then do it."

Lori thought Dr. Sitz would strangle Owen, if only Owen didn't have thick shoulders and tree-trunk thighs. His baggy corduroys and loose flannel shirt concealed raw, mulish strength that she imagined could lift cars. Other nurses thought Owen a little slow. Lori enjoyed his good cheer but found it unsettling too, considering his father's rapid decline from healthy sixty-year-old widower to mostly dead ICU patient.

No other crash-cart saviors had charged into Mr. Smiley's room. She, alone, captured V-fib waves worming across the monitor screen, caught death in the act. Instinctively she struck Mr. Smiley's sternum with the fleshy part of her fist. This year she was forever tired and had stopped going to the gym, but the thud was surprisingly loud, her thirty extra pounds put to good use. The alarms paused. A train of steady beeps celebrated his successful return to a state of perpetual dying.

Her motivations left her uneasy. Did she want to save Mr. Smiley or rough up death a little? How much did it matter? Her actions were arguably the only successful intervention in Mr. Smiley's care.

Lori felt sorry for patients like Mr. Smiley, those described as going downhill fast. Four weeks earlier, when informed he had appendicitis, Mr. Smiley told the surgeon on-call for the ED to get it out and get him home. A postoperative abscess complicated the uneventful surgery. The antibiotics treating the abscess caused C. difficile colitis, an inflammation of the colon. During surgery to remove part of the colon, Mr. Smiley suffered a heart attack and cardiac arrest and never regained consciousness.

"Complication dominoes," Lori overhead the residents and nurses say. "He's circling the drain." Many avoided his room, as if misfortune was contagious.

When visiting hours began, Owen stood waiting outside the ICU as he did every morning, with a Great One coffee, a dozen donuts, and two daily papers. He and Lori exchanged polite smiles. Nobody else ever visited Mr. Smiley. Owen stayed all day.

Dr. Sitz explained what had happened and pointed to Lori. "You have *that* nurse to thank," he said. Lori couldn't decide whether his tone carried praise or condemnation.

Afterward, Freckles pulled her aside. "You need to be more careful," she said.

.   .   .

"Watch out for Freckles," Tess warned her that evening as she seared two steaks in Lori's kitchen.

"What can she do?" Lori said. "I did the right thing for my patient."

"Being responsible," Tess said. "Doesn't protect you from being fucked with."

They became best friends in nursing school twenty years earlier. Tess had been Lori's only choice to be David's godmother. Over the years, Tess had bought him his first baseball mitt and tennis racket, and once in college, after he began dating his girlfriend, a copy of *Our Bodies, Ourselves*. She promised to keep fresh roses at David's roadside cross. Only twelve miles away, Lori couldn't steel herself to visit the crash site. Three separate times she came close. Inside a block, though, her imagination stormed. She felt his ribs snap, spleen rupture. Rage and self-pity replaced blood in her body and her legs couldn't support that much weight.

After Tess left, Lori cleaned the kitchen, showered, and tried to read in bed. Then the phone rang. "I hope I didn't wake you," said the judge.

"Do I have to call the cops? Stop harassing me."

"Don't think that, Lori. I want you to forgive me."

"Are you fucking crazy?"

"I feel awful, Lori. If there's anything I can do, you must ask. I mean it."

"Yeah? I'll keep that in mind."

"Do that, please." She heard him ordering cheeseburgers, fries, and a large coke.

"You're driving?"

"I am."

"But you're drunk. Don't lie to me."

"I respect you too much to lie."

"You killed my son." She swallowed hard. "Doesn't it make you want to change?"

"Sure," the judge said. "But it's a far away want. You can't just put it on your to-do list and cross it off. Besides, I wasn't drunk at the time of the accident."

"Your blood alcohol level was over 400. The lab work showed it."

"That's protected information. False but confidential. I can bring a lot of trouble to you and the person who disclosed it. But I know you're not thinking clearly. " Lori heard him chewing, then slurping the bottom of a drink. "I must go," he said.

.   .   .

The next morning, Lori was reminded to be grateful that the ICU was three floors up from the ED. A young father, a high school chemistry teacher, stopped by the ED for flu-like symptoms and coded in the waiting room. Lori had transferred to the ICU believing it would help her cope with David's death. Here, death was rarely sudden, arbitrary, and unexpected. Death was buffered. Making patients comfortable was an end to a deliberate process. It wasn't less tragic for family and friends, but it was easier for her.

A pulse and blood pressure returned, but the young father was critical, suffering from severe myocarditis, an inflammation of the heart muscle. But there was no room in the ICU. All the beds were occupied. Dr. Sitz decided to make Mr. Smiley comfortable and called Owen at home to inform him. "Don't," said Owen, his voice throwing sparks. "I'm on my way."

Owen hurried through the ICU, bearing his usual Great One, donuts, and newspapers. He waved to his father, nodded to Lori, and made camp on a wheeled tray table as if it was another typical morning.

Dr. Sitz strode into the room. His narrow face and sharp nose were focused to a hard point. His prematurely gray hair, usually combed neatly to the side, fell over eyes dulled from exhaustion.

"We can't treat your father indefinitely."

"Why not?"

"It's futile," Dr. Sitz said. "I told you that."

"What do you mean, futile?"

"What have we been talking about the past few days? Futile. From the Greek word *futilis*. It means brittle, leaks easily. It means your father will never get better."

Lori's jaw dropped. She thought she could hear the tumblers clicking in Owen's mind as he made sense of futile and *futilis*. Dr. Sitz waited, arms crossed over his wrinkled scrub top. Lori noticed drops of blood on the goggles hanging from his neck.

Owen opened the box, found a jelly donut. "You're saying he's better off dead?"

"He won't recover. He's suffering terribly. What kind of life is that?" asked Dr. Sitz, gesturing to Mr. Smiley.

"A quiet life," said Owen. Lori weighed the alternative tragedies. To have a loved one ripped away without warning, or forced to witness the slow assault by disease and technology.

"The surgeon made him like this, and you haven't fixed him."

Dr. Sitz dug his thumbs into the circles sagging beneath his eyes.

"That he's not getting better doesn't mean we've done anything wrong. Sometimes the disease wins," Dr. Sitz said and stormed from the room.

Owen's face was ashen. The box trembled when he offered Lori a donut. After hanging one of Mr. Smiley's three antibiotics, Lori accepted a jelly on a paper towel.

"This is a good donut," she said.

Owen smiled shyly. "They go stale real quick."

"You must get them first thing in the morning," said Lori.

"Yes. You know," Owen said, chewing slowly, eyes bright and companionable.

"How are you holding up?" Lori asked.

"It's only me and him," Owen confessed. "My mother died three years ago. A bleeding ulcer, they said. She was a nurse in this hospital. Alice Smiley."

Lori remembered working with Alice Smiley as a young nursing intern. Heavy makeup, long sleeves under scrubs even in the dog days of summer, forever cheery. Lori wondered if Owen's daily vigils were attempts to get closer to her memory.

"It must be scary to be alone," Lori said.

She stared at Mr. Smiley—skin the color of chicken fat, gooped-up eyes, bloated body, rising and falling to the rhythm of the ventilator. Owen never asked about his father's condition. He agreed freely to Dr. Sitz's plans, never questioning until now.

"Do you have kids, Lori?" asked Owen.

Lori's eyes floated to the bangs of his hair. Cut coarsely, as if done in a mirror. His entire body seemed pasted together: large head, big hands, and shoes like rowboats.

"I don't," she said.

"Too bad," he said. "You seem like somebody who'd be a good mother."

Lori licked the sugar off her fingertips. "Time to get back to work," she said.

"He used to say I was slow," said Owen. "He called me a tard."

Lori restlessly dabbed Mr. Smiley's forehead with a damp cloth. He was helpless in his decay. He was her patient, her responsibility. He belonged to her.

"When he lost the store, he blamed me. My mother's death was my fault, too. Caring for me was too much for her. When she died, he said, 'Look what you did!'"

Lori wiped Mr. Smiley's chin. Maybe vengeance, and not love, drove Owen to keep his father alive, and lingering between suffering and death was entirely the point.

Dr. Sitz entered the room again, sat down, smacked his knees.

"Leave him alone," howled Owen.

Dr. Sitz pinched his eyes. "He's had his chance. Let someone else have a turn."

"Why should I care about anyone else?" said Owen. "Nobody cares about me."

Dr. Sitz looked at Lori. She prodded him to answer.

"All this isn't yours to use at will," Dr. Sitz said to Owen, gesturing to the bed, the machines, the nurses and staff staring at him. "Nobody lives in the ICU. Patients get better and leave, or they die."

Owen stammered, stared into the donut box as if help could be found there.

"A young man just died in the ER," said Dr. Sitz. "If I had gotten him up here he might have lived. A young boy will now grow up without his father."

Owen's eyes reddened. Lori wanted to lay her arm around his shoulder, create space between herself and Dr. Sitz, whose words were accurate but cold. She remained silent and stone-like. After all, it will be her hands pushing the drugs.

"I'm writing the order to make your father comfortable," said Dr. Sitz.

Owen frantically tossed his empty coffee cup in the donut box, collected his newspapers under his arm, and bustled out the room.

Dr. Sitz gestured for Lori to gather the necessary medications.

"Not this time," said Lori.

"I'm the doctor," said Dr. Sitz. "I'm the one ultimately responsible."

Lori looked up from charting, smiled tensely. The sparse room was chilling. No silly or flowery cards, no silver "Get Well" balloons, no colorful but crude drawings from grandkids. "Mr. Smiley is my patient, too," she said.

"C'mon, Lori. Caring for someone who won't get better can't feel good."

"If I only cared for patients with a good prognosis, I wouldn't be caring for many patients. Especially here." She stopped writing. "You never stay in the room after ordering a patient to be made comfortable. Why is that? And give me a real answer."

Dr. Sitz slouched down in the chair, set his chin on his chest. "This decision is hard. It would be impossible if I had to watch."

She flinched, startled by his honesty.

"I'm not obligated to provide useless care. It's fraud."

"His son has hope," said Lori. "Irrational hope, but isn't that worth something?"

"You're saying there's value in mistaken beliefs?"

"Who's making that judgment?" asked Lori. "You were fine with Owen when he agreed with the treatment plan. Now he disagrees, and that means he's crazy?"

"OK, not crazy. But his elevator doesn't go all the way to the top."

"Perhaps," said Lori. "But does it go high enough?"

Dr. Sitz shifted restlessly. "His elevator doesn't matter anymore."

Lori knew better than to tell someone there wasn't hope without being certain what that person was hoping for. She'd been living off irrational hope the past year. David's death felt absurd. Her amazing boy had been reduced to a cliché, a statistic, another cross at the side of the road. She hoped the absurd circumstances of his death would thin out, permitting memories of his life to reemerge in vivid detail.

"You can't make Mr. Smiley comfortable with Owen off somewhere."

"We need the bed."

"The whole thing hurts."

"What am I supposed to do?" Dr. Sitz asked.

"Get Freckles. Find another nurse. Do it yourself. Maybe you won't do it at all."

.   .   .

Lori was driving home, the middle lane on I-95, focusing on what her headlights allowed, when a woman on a cell phone plowed into her lane. Lori leaned on the horn. The woman didn't offer an apologetic wave. She kept talking and changing lanes as if the other vehicles, and the people inside them, didn't exist. Lori gunned the gas to catch her. Then what? She imagined David watching, didn't want to embarrass herself for revenge, an impulse with an extremely short half-life.

She returned home, relieved to find Tess sitting in the kitchen, sipping red wine and making a veal stew, David's favorite meal.

"What are you doing?"

"We're celebrating David," said Tess.

Lori smiled kindly, but didn't talk about her son, voice any emotion, or even submit to the occasion. She described her near accident.

"The world is made of the inconsiderate selfish and those who must look out for them," Tess said, pouring Lori a glass of wine.

"I feel so powerless," Lori said. "I must do something. But what?"

Tess clinked their wine glasses. "You eat. You drink. You laugh."

Lori offered a toast of thanks for the meal, but only picked at her plate. Part of her wished to be alone, only she couldn't identify which part that was, and if it could be trusted.

"I think I'll stay here tonight," said Tess. "I'll curl up on the couch." She held up the wine bottle. "If you're not going to help with this, more for me."

. . .

Later, the clock on Lori's nightstand read 11:27 P.M. Lori called down to Tess. "I haven't heard from the judge. Nothing."

"Maybe he's in a ditch somewhere," Tess yelled back upstairs.

"What about drinking and eating and laughing?"

"Symptom management only," Tess said, then paused. "Wine makes me honest, and I finished off the bottle." Lori felt the silence take on an electric charge. "You've dealt with David's death so well, maybe too well."

"Yeah, right," Lori thought. She refused to let on to her closest friend how low she had sunk. She had hit bottom and pushed through, emerging into an alternate reality that looked miraculously like the old one. In this new place her chest wasn't crushed by sadness; it only ached. She could breathe, think and cradle contradictions. She could pine for a call from the judge and at the same time wish he was bloodied, decapitated, and wrapped around a telephone pole. And when the doorbell rang a few hours deeper into the night, every parent's nightmare, she jumped awake. But David was already dead. She chuckled and almost cried.

There were voices downstairs. She crouched at the top of the stairs, angled a view through slats in the banisters. Filling the doorframe was a tall, handsome man, gray hair trimmed above the ears. He wore a dark suit, a striped tie loose at the neck. He held a dozen roses, each individually wrapped in plastic, the type sold in all night bodegas. When he gave them to Tess there were tears in his eyes. "I'm sorry, Lori."

Lori instantly recognized his voice.

The judge mistook Tess for Lori, and Tess was following along. Lori had dreams where she confronted him, clawed away his skin and showered him with acid. But seeing him, and not thinking about him, had tamed her rage. She wanted him to leave so she could restore the barbaric hatred he deserved.

"I don't know how it happened," he said, voice clogged with tears.

Tess buried her face into the roses—the petals must smell like the plastic that kept its shape, Lori thought. Tess admired the bouquet like it was a newborn infant. Too fragile and melodramatic, Lori wanted to yell at her. Get it right. But she couldn't say which gestures and feelings were the right ones when she hadn't been close enough to her own grief.

"I'm a person with a degree of power," he said, almost apologetically. "If I could give you your son back, I would. You must believe that."

Tess placed her hand on the judge's shoulder. He winced. Lori white-knuckled the rail, eyes bulging through the banister slats. She wanted to strangle them both. She watched herself pushing the judge away, telling him to get home safe. The door shut and locked on a man still pleading his case. Dry-eyed, she saw herself sobbing from that place she had yet to find.

. . .

Early the next morning, the first anniversary of David's death, Tess and the roses were gone. Lori drove to the block beyond which she could never pass. Her heart was jumping; her body was shaking. She couldn't tell if the emotions bringing a cold fever to her skin was great courage or terrible shame. She parked with a soft but surprising jump of the curb, a lilt of the tire felt only after it slipped down. David did this when she was teaching him how to parallel park. "That's a helluva place to put a curb," he said. She thought it a joke and was poised to snuff his teenage flippancy, when she noticed his tremulous hands gripping the wheel. She encouraged him to give it another try, only this time cut the wheel sooner. He didn't move, head hung low. "C'mon," she said. "And I'll see who's responsible for that curb."

Lori shut the engine in the middle of that memory and was quick-stepping on the sidewalk before she thought too hard on it. She picked up the pace, lengthened her strides. Soon she was breathing hard, building momentum, emptying her head, riding a rhythm. Then she tripped on a gaping buckle in the sidewalk. She gasped, stumbled forward, certain her teeth would be crushed by concrete. But she steadied herself, remained on her feet. Catching her breath, she looked around to see if anyone had witnessed this graceless moment, when she saw the roses leaning among the crocuses at the foot of

David's roadside cross. She wasn't religious, but the cross was squared, like the symbol for the Red Cross, so she didn't mind it.

She also discovered she wasn't alone. The Escalade was parked across the street. The judge was fast asleep behind the wheel, drool and dew on the driver's side window. She knocked on the window. His flat face moved against the glass. An eye opened, a weary, washed-out blue. She waved at him, a haunting wave, a recognition from afar.

She stood at the cross waiting for the tears, the sound of smashing metal, waves of anger and rage. She pulled a few weeds, propped up the roses. She inhaled the morning, waited a little longer, listened to a dog barking in the distance, then drove to work.

.   .   .

Owen arrived at his usual time, offered donuts to everyone sneering at him, including Dr. Sitz, who refused at first, then picked up a powdered cruller.

"We're setting up," Dr. Sitz said. "Would you like a few minutes alone?'

Owen ran to his father's bedside. "You can't touch him."

Owen gulped at the sight of the security guard in the doorway, which surprised Lori.

"I don't know how I'll live after he's gone," said Owen.

"What were you doing before he got sick?" asked Lori.

She had accepted his constant presence without thinking how he squared long hours at the hospital with a regular job. Owen looked at everyone waiting for his answer.

Lori stared at Mr. Smiley, dependent on drugs and machines for every breath, for sustaining the weakest of blood pressures. But there was one thing Mr. Smiley could do, she realized, simply by not being dead.

"His social security checks," she said. "That's why you need to keep him alive."

Owen's head hung as if she snapped his neck. His arms fell to his side.

Lori spun away from him, flushed with disgust.

"Do you want to stay?" Dr. Sitz asked Owen, who turned and shuffled out.

Dr. Sitz raised one of the syringes. Lori thought his movements too slow, his breathing too quick. Freckles arrived and asked what was taking so long. Lori grabbed the syringe from Dr. Sitz. There was a hole in the ritual where dignity and respect belonged. Her hands cared for Mr. Smiley, and only from her hands could this act be considered part of that care.

She worked methodically. Dr. Sitz remained at the bedside. His color paled as the drugs moved through the IV tubing into Mr. Smiley's veins. The waves dancing across the heart monitor slowed, then kneeled and crawled, and finally laid down flat. Dr. Sitz bit his lip, closed his eyes.

Lori found Owen slumped in the ICU waiting room.

"Can I get you anything?"

"Coffee. I want coffee. Please."

She called the cafeteria, ordered up four coffees: one for Owen and herself, one for Freckles and Dr. Sitz. Lori sat beside Owen, who considered the small size of the Styrofoam coffee cup with a bemused expression. "What's wrong?" Lori said.

"Nothing." He sighed contentedly with each sip. "I usually spill this much."

Lori imagined herself inside his inscrutable mind. Keeping Mr. Smiley alive reeked of manipulation, selfishness, and necessity. She understood, but couldn't accept, what Owen had done.

She cleaned Mr. Smiley's body, made sure the sheets were fresh and a stiff, starched white. She sensed David's wiry body over her shoulder and wished she would cry. Had he survived, he would have forgiven the judge. Her hatred for the judge was growing sympathy, but she needed the hatred. Without it, she faced the full thrust of her grief, the severity of how much she missed her son.

6

Rainbow

"Why me? I'm stuck in the ER all day and he's on the couch watching football."

"Please go back to your room," I said, my voice rising. "How many times have we asked you?"

Her boyfriend had thrown her tall, spidery frame to the floor in their house, part of a two-family dwelling that EMS quipped was on the fire department's "Let Burn" list. He'd choked her and yanked out a tuft of hair, leaving a divot in her blunt bangs. She'd tried to kick out the window of the police cruiser en route to the emergency department. In the ED, she appeared girlish and forgivable in her oversized hoodie, gnashing her fingernails, idling tearfully. Her pacing and shotgun blaming of the world could be heard by everyone. These outbursts were punctuated by frequent visits to the central desk where the unit clerk and nurses were trying to work, drawing other patients and their visitors out from behind curtains and doors to complain and rubberneck.

"Be respectful of other patients," I said to her.

"I'm sorry," she said, slapping tears from strong cheekbones, snapping back to her room as obediently as a bungee cord. "But why do *I* have to suffer?"

Everyone thought her remarkably beautiful for a woman in her forties, until we learned she was twenty-eight.

"I made him a sandwich. I paid for the drugs with my money. He never made me a sandwich. Never."

"You want a sandwich?" I asked.

"I want a sandwich."

"We can do that. Is turkey OK?"

We only had turkey on white bread, though each was wrapped with packets of mayo and mustard; well-intentioned but limited options, similar to the solace and assurance we offered her.

"If I speak when I'm not supposed to speak, he hits me. If I buy chunky peanut butter, he hits me. Sometimes he just hits me. For breathing. What the hell? I can't fucking breathe?"

Finding sympathy for her was easy; feeling sympathy was harder. She was a diligent and responsible consumer of alcohol and crack, as well as marijuana four times a day to balance out the cocaine. She didn't take her psychiatric medications. "Why?" I asked.

"Everyone knows you shouldn't mix psych meds with booze and coke. I'm not *that* crazy."

"Wouldn't a better choice be to stop the alcohol and cocaine?" I asked.

The pupils of her dark eyes dilated with deep thought. "Maybe. My psychiatrist doesn't know what she's doing. The meds zombie me out."

A neighbor called police. When they arrived, she wouldn't press charges. "It'll make the hitting worse," she said.

"You might come back in a body bag," I said to her.

"Yes," she said, jumping excitingly in her chair, as if I'd solved a gnawing riddle and not raised concern for her safety. "He told me many times he'd kill me if he knew he wouldn't get caught."

"Doesn't that worry you?" I ask.

"It takes a lot to kill a person," she said. She pushed up her sleeve and flexed a long, taut bicep inked with tattoos. "I can handle myself. I grew up with brothers."

She called home. Her mother wouldn't talk to her. One brother, then another, cursed at her and said they were locking the front door if she showed up.

After an hour with her, the psychiatric social worker emerged dull eyed. She recited a liturgy of diagnoses listed in her file: depression, bipolar, dependent personality disorder, histrionic. But there was little justification for holding her. She didn't pose an immediate and imminent harm to herself or others. Her self-destructive habits consistently contradicted her best interests, and yet, what was safety to such a person, living such a life?

I didn't know what to do with her boyfriend's alleged homicidal threats. The police said they were called to intervene in their domestic disturbances all the time.

A call to the domestic violence hotline brought the prompt arrival of an eager volunteer, who, after a long conversation, surfaced from the room massaging her temples and arranged emergency placement in a women's shelter. We breathed relief. Not a solution, but a respite, and sometimes that counts as a victory.

Only she refused. The shelter didn't allow dogs.

Thinking about her dog set off more tears, another blitz to the nursing station. "I have to get my dog. I have to get Rainbow."

"Where's Rainbow?"

"With my boyfriend."

Our mouths dropped open in choked silence.

"I have a plan. I'll pick up Rainbow, then drive to my mom."

"Your mother won't talk with you. Your boyfriend beat you up," I reminded her. "The shelter might be the best thing for tonight. Tomorrow you can rethink your options."

"No." She asked to call her boyfriend and snatched the receiver at the desk.

"Tie Rainbow to the porch," she said to her boyfriend. "Yes, I'm coming to get him. What? Why not? No, Rainbow is *my* dog."

She smacked the phone into the cradle.

"He said I have to come through the front door if I want Rainbow." Her fingers blindly prettied her hair. "He's my dog," she announced to us. We understood. We owned dogs, too. Determination and purpose flushed her face. "I can use another turkey sandwich." We gave her two. She stuffed her cheeks to bulging with one sandwich and pushed the other into the hand warmer of her hoodie. "For Rainbow."

She drew back her narrow shoulders, and charged off without waiting to be discharged, leaving behind a bruised quiet and uncomfortable relief.

7

The Telephone Pole

Everyone leaves—the medics, the police, the coroner, the late night news crew—and Gabe unpacks the camera and focuses the lens on the tread marks, the telephone pole, the crushed SUV and the indestructible vodka bottle wedged into the front seat. The scalp remains where they found it, hanging from the shattered windshield. Gabe's gut contracts. The sweat starts up again. The neon yellow Bureau of Roads Protection shirt, a toxic polyester, now itches his back without mercy. New to the job, Gabe suspects the scalp was abandoned by the boys as part of an initiation prank. He turns the lens to the bank of the road, to daylight sneaking up behind the clouds, but his sympathies return to the scalp. His knees weaken. He feels nothing for the scalped driver, a prominent judge entangled in an alcohol-related crash two years earlier; one where a college freshman was killed.

"Drunk driving was never proven," says Shep, his boss at the Bureau of Roads Protection and his brother-in-law, when he calls Gabe's cell to check on him.

"The judge got zero punishment," says Gabe. "Bad press, that's all."

"Poor guy broke three ribs," Shep says. "He was handed a shitload of pain."

"A young man died."

"A tragedy."

"And if he had killed Oliver instead of that boy. Or Blaze? If one of our boys happened to be on the receiving end of his tragedy?"

"You need to focus. What's past is past," says Shep.

"Shakespeare wrote 'What's past is prologue,'" says Gabe.

Shep coughs into the phone. "Luckily Shakespeare never worked for the Bureau of Roads Protection. Can you have a preliminary report to me by lunch?"

"Brunch," Gabe says. "No problem."

"Who's better than you?"

Gabe hangs up, slips the phone into his vest pocket and steps closer to the scalp. Closer scrutiny reveals what's most troubling about the divot of silver hair: it doesn't seem out of place. No longer bleeding, it sways in the breeze as if it naturally grows there, has no choice but to grow there. Perhaps the coroner had reached a similarly twisted conclusion, Gabe reconsiders, and purposefully left the scalp where it now asserted itself.

Daybreak finds Gabe completing field sketches. Back at the office, he analyzes the fatal crash scene, scribbles pages of calculations. He rules out illumination, road conditions, and weather. Fatigue wraps itself around his aching bones when his report, padded with computer simulation, lands on Shep's desk. He concludes that human factors were responsible, speed was a consideration, and the influence of alcohol wasn't insignificant.

.   .   .

A chill drips along Gabe's spine the next morning after Shep informs him about an urgent request to appear before the State Committee on Automotive Mishaps (SCAM). This quirky state he now calls home has been a perpetual source of fascination, bafflement, and ulcer-stoking angst. It was a crucible of contradictory elements, stocked with breathless coastlines and bright donut shops, great universities and weak public schools, old industrial work ethic and crippling unemployment, low-key friendliness and good-natured disregard for one of the highest drunk driving mortality rates, per capita, in the country.

The latter problem spurred the governor to create the position of Accident Reconstructionist in Shep's Bureau of Roads Protection, which operates under SCAM in ways that Gabe was discovering in his first months on the job in this new world. A popular teacher in the Department of Engineering and Physical Sciences at the local college, Gabe resigned when denied tenure. His chairman expressed terrible regrets, but Gabe thought the sentiment well intentioned but hollow. Shep hired him despite accusations of nepotism. Gabe's CV quieted the loudest critics. This state job demanded a certain education and skill set, one that most people with political ties, born and raised and schooled in the state, sorely lacked.

"What government committee has meetings in a coffee shop?" he asks Ellen.

"One that knows the best coffee in the state."

She and Shep were natives, high school sports legends, and evangelical in their local pride. "Relax. Shep will be there."

Stan Bigly, SCAM's chairman, pops up from a group of men huddled around two round café tables pulled together and greets Gabe with a bone-crushing handshake.

"What's your poison? Cappuccino? Latte?"

"Tea."

"Tea?" Stan Bigly's dental work and overbite combine in such a way that makes Gabe feel silly. He reaches for his wallet. Stan waves him off. "Sit. We have an account here." A younger man sporting a dark suit similar to the other men at the table ignores the line stretching out the entrance and catches the eye of the tattooed server. He yells at Stan Bigly, who taps Gabe on the shoulder. "You want a biscotti, or maybe a cookie? They have great cookies here."

"I'm fine, thanks," says Gabe, finding this scene recognizable but unreal.

"Your report displays obvious intelligence," says Stan Bigly.

Gabe smiles. Stan Bigly rubs his tortoise face. "But you ignored the core issue."

"I included everything relevant to the crash."

"Except that we have a rogue telephone pole problem on Route 6."

"Excuse me?" Gabe shoots a look at Shep, who opens his face, an expression Gabe doesn't know what to do with. "The judge was drunk. We have a drunk driving problem."

Stan Bigly grins painfully at Gabe. "Have you ever been here?"

Gabe shakes his head, feeling lesser for it.

"Take a look. People reading the paper before work, powerbrokers and lawyers, medics, hipsters, a smattering of ne'er-do-wells, college students studying books with titles I don't understand. This crowd of geniuses, leaders, future leaders, past leaders, working Joe's, fuck-ups, and future fuck-ups share a common purpose for being here. Is it love of excellent coffee? Fuck, no. Though I dare you to find a better cup elsewhere. It's a need for belonging, for community. That's the essence of this place. And now you're here, Gabe, a citizen of the coffee shop."

Gabe was once a citizen of Canada. He had crossed the border permanently eighteen years earlier, after marrying Ellen and leaving the University of Toronto to finish his PhD dissertation in Boston. Despite the taxes he's paid, the hours coaching Oliver's Little League teams, and later his son's middle school math team, he still feels an outsider in this state where natives cross-pollinate as children. Stan Bigly was a high school buddy of the governor, and Shep played football with Bigly's younger brother. The governor appointed the members of SCAM, a group of mysterious purpose, but one with health benefits and a pension.

Stan Bigly brushes up tabletop crumbs before placing a large coffee, and not a tea, before Gabe. "This kills me," he says. "People can't treat public spaces with respect?"

"Are you treating poles with respect?" Gabe paused. "Accusing them of murder?"

The committee members raise their collective eyes from their Blackberries and shake their heads; their hair colored the same shade of black, skin thickened with the same Florida tan, disappointment razored with the same pity.

"The judge is only one incident," says Stan Bigly. "There have been six deaths in the last two months alone."

"Alcohol played a major role in each of them," Gabe says.

"So was that pole," says Stan Bigly, who owns several popular bars.

"We *have* a pole problem," says Shep, injecting himself into the conversation. "I know it. You know it. And Gabe knows the judge didn't die a senseless death."

Stan Bigly stands, pulls Gabe up with him. "Put yourself in these people's shoes. Bars serve a public good. They bring people together. Just like coffee shops."

Gabe nods as if his neck is in spasm. The young man in the suit leers at him, then cracks an unfriendly smile. The mistaken coffee for tea was a purposeful accident. A tense minute of silence follows, and soon Gabe understands the meeting to be over.

.   .   .

"You didn't have my back, Shep," says Gabe. "I did a good job. A damn good job." He searches Ellen's face for support. She's busy tossing salad, staring at her big brother.

"Solid work. Definitely," says Shep, picking the label off his beer bottle.

"Be straight with me," says Gabe.

Ellen slices a freshly baked loaf of olive bread. The knife knocking cautionary warnings on the cutting board, lest Gabe forget his nine jobless months shooting resumes into a black hole, her phys ed teacher paycheck and stipend for coaching girls' soccer stretching only so far. Hope was running on fumes before Shep secured him this job.

"What's the problem, Shep?" says Gabe. "I see we have a problem."

Shep musses his blonde hair, retreats behind dimples and white teeth. Still the surfer, though thick in the face and gut. Shep would have charmed the Tenure Committee into a promotion, Gabe believed, despite the little fact that he dropped out of college.

"Have you thought about the judge's family," says Shep. "His wife and three boys?"

"I was hired to reconstruct accidents, perform root cause analysis, and improve the safety of the roads."

Ellen calls up the stairs for Oliver to put down his homework and join them for dinner. Gabe sets the table with ill temper. He notices she's limping again as she returns.

"The hip is still bothering you?" he whispers to her.

Ellen's face is stiff. Gabe can't decide whether it reflects her serious intent on this issue, a willful resistance to his question, or the pain she's fighting and trying to conceal.

"I want safer roads, too," says Shep.

"We all do," says Ellen.

"But the poles are at fault?" Gabe studies his wife. "You believe this?"

"We must keep an open mind, and not be quick to judge," says Ellen.

"Judge the judge?" says Shep.

Ellen laughs as she pours the wine. "Come, let's eat."

.   .   .

The headline above the fold in the morning paper states "Telephone Poles Open Hunting Season." Below it a picture of Stan Bigly at a news conference after the judge's memorial service. "Telephone poles are preying on drivers exercising their right to intoxicated self-expression," he said. "Poles don't want us returning to our loving families after a bottle of wine with dinner or one last round with our buddies."

A sidebar describes one reporter's attempts to get a response from Lori Davis, the mother of the boy killed by the judge years before. An ICU nurse, she was stopped outside the hospital after an evening shift. "No, this isn't justice," she says. "When someone dies, the family suffers most."

Ellen drops the spoon from her yogurt and sliced fruit as he reads the word "dies." The unspoken prospect of mortality has been floating in the air the past few weeks, ever since a routine right hip X-ray for unexplained pain revealed what her doctor described as a bone lucency of uncertain significance. When Gabe asked the doctor if the lucency meant cancer, Ellen didn't allow her to finish. "I run twenty-eight miles a week."

"Not anymore," said Gabe. "What's the next step, doc?" he asked.

"I eat great," Ellen said. "Even my vices are healthy—red wine and dark chocolate."

"A bone scan would be recommended," said the doctor.

Ellen's blue eyes widened. "Who wants to challenge me to push-ups?"

Gabe later cruised the Internet and found too much information and not enough answers. He thought lucency meant clarity, but in radiological terms it signified absence. Normal bone appeared white on X-ray because it was opaque and the beams didn't penetrate. Any loss of bone structure allowed the X-ray beam to travel through. These areas appeared dark or black—a lucency—on the film. A bone lucency appeared empty, but Gabe learned they harbored many meanings, from benign cysts to an endless palette of haunting cancers.

.   .   .

Gabe can't sleep. Telephone poles coming to life. His wife pacing the room, thumping the floor to find that space unoccupied by pain.

"Can I get you anything?" he asks. "Tylenol, ibuprofen, an ambulance?"

"Go to sleep," she snaps. He's disarmed by this outburst, a new piece to her personality. He suspects it isn't his desire to help that upset her, but his witnessing of a moment she believes to be, needs to be, private.

He shuts his eyes and listens, endures her enduring.

"I'm fine," she says. "Too much walking the past few days. I thought exercise might do some good."

"That doesn't explain the spot on the X-ray," he says, as if talking in his sleep.

"If not for the X-ray, we wouldn't know about it, and you'd agree that all the walking might have something to do with the pain."

"So you admit to having pain?"

"An ache. More like a stiffness."

Her resistance irritates him, grates at his sympathy, and he's about to tell her this when his cell phone goes off. He curses the phone, the ungodly time, the thwarted sleep.

"Get up and get here," says Shep.

"Hello to you, too," says Gabe.

"The pole on Route 6 again. Tyffany Hynds, young single mother barhopping with friends. We must respond to this, right now."

"Shit," says Gabe, and hangs up. He rubs his eyes, swings his legs up out of bed, and yawns. Why dream, he thinks, when reality feels like a hallucination?

.   .   .

Gabe trawls the ground surrounding the pole. He screws his face into serious-ness, takes a wooden tongue blade and wedges it between the pole and hard dirt. "There's no gap, no tilt to the soil," he says, as if citing a genuine discovery.

"What are you saying?" says Shep.

"There is no evidence the pole moved."

"Find some," said Shep.

Gabe settles in, takes photographs and measurements, draws sketches with painstaking detail. The stink of burnt rubber and gasoline fumes, the bitter sweetness of pear tree blossoms, gives Gabe a headache. If springtime ever gave up, let itself go, stopped showering and hit the bottle, this is what it might smell like.

Gabe spots a reporter, the mother of one of Oliver's friends, interviewing Shep.

"Records show the driver had a suboptimal pole encounter two weeks ago."

"I don't think this is a coincidence," says Shep.

"How worried should the public be?" the reporter asks.

"This is a tragedy," says Shep. "Our sympathies to Tyffany Hynds's family. They should know my team at the Bureau of Roads Protection is investigating."

The reporter snatches Gabe's sleeve. "Any comments, Gabe? Tell us, why are telephone poles targeting drunk drivers and sparing the sober ones?"

Lost in the unreality of the moment, he stares deep into the camera. He sees Ellen, a former collegiate soccer player, limping about their bedroom like a felled lion, fashioned in his collared shirt and her rationalizations. The possibility that poles can move, that she can caulk the lucency in her hip by will alone, smacks of courage and fear, a belief in modern fairy tales, which Gabe finds romantic, unhealthy, and ultimately absurd.

"We haven't found evidence suggesting threatening pole behavior." Gabe speaks into the camera, his frustration targeted at his wife. "Or that poles possess *any* behavior."

"Two pole attacks in two weeks," says Tyffany Hynds's father, when informed of Gabe's comment. "They were stalking my daughter." Her children, two pre-schoolers, cling to his leg. Tears swell the eyes of a man possessing the heft and desperation of a mobile home. "Is he telling me it's my little girl's fault?"

.   .   .

Gabe drops the report on Shep's desk knowing full well that data fails to capture the essence of the crash. Sleep sits behind his eyes, forces him home for a quick rest. He finds two neighbors stomping the sidewalk in front of his driveway. Chants of "Pole Sympathizer" echo beneath the leafy oaks shading his otherwise quiet street.

"What the hell?" he says to Sid and his son, Charlie.

Sid constructs a grin out of white skin, neck fat, and light green eyes. "You're looking at the founder and president of the new neighborhood chapter of D3."

"D3?"

"Drunks for Drunk Driving."

"Weren't you in AA?"

"The definition of addiction includes relapse."

"Damn it, Sid," says Gabe, wishing his brain didn't feel like a wet rag. "I'm sorry you can't find work. I really am. But don't you have anything better to do?"

"We saw you on the morning news," says Charlie. "Folks are pissed."

"Oh really? Well, I'm pissed," says Gabe.

From the back pocket of his loose jeans, Sid pulls out the morning paper. He reads the headline aloud as if a formal decree: "Poles Falsely Accused."

Gabe grabs the paper from Sid's hands. Below the headline sits his photo. Gabe bites his lip. The night before he was aware that he was speaking into a camera, but the moment felt like harmless chatter.

"Go back to Canada," yells Charlie.

Gabe shakes his head. Awarded the "No Child Left Behind Junior Scholar" citation at high school graduation two years before, Charlie now lives with Sid.

"Do you know where Canada is?" Gabe asks Charlie.

"Next to Toronto," Charlie answers.

Sid lowers his head, a father weakened, his love bleeding pride.

Gabe's eyes seize upon the washed-out color photograph on Charlie's placard. He angles closer, squints against the sun. "Is that a fetus?"

"Abortion clinic doesn't open until 9 A.M.," says Charlie.

"You can't protest outside my house.

"Let's ask the First Amendment," says Sid.

Gabe hangs his head, unable to resist sleep or refute Sid's reasoning. He nods at the placard. "At least use proper imagery. You're misrepresenting your problem with me." Sid bobs his head, conceding a point well made.

.   .   .

Gabe stakes out the pole on Route 6 the next night. He sets up a video camera, lines the pole's base with white chalk. Stan Bigly isn't happy with Gabe's comments and orders Shep to find irrefutable proof. Gabe now sinks shamefully into the peaceful, front seat discomfort of his government sedan. He's waiting for a fatal crash. The proof he needs demands that another person die. He listens to the radio. He hums along to "Blue Bayou," a dedication from Mae in Albany, who wants to start over with her ex-boyfriend. "Go get him, Mae," he cheers, guilt-ridden for leaving his wife and her inscrutable night aches to watch a pole not move.

.   .   .

Gabe returns home to find Sid and Charlie demonstrating again. Their placards now scream "Pole Lover" in red and black strokes. Worry works into Gabe's bones.

"Are you happy?" says Sid as Gabe slumps by.

"Encouraged," says Gabe, fighting the sun. "We're getting somewhere."

"Where's that?" says Charlie.

"We'll know once we get there."

.   .   .

Shep joins him on the stakeout the following night. Gabe frets about his brother-in-law's true motives. But Shep jabbers on about his ex-wife, his child support high colonic, and Blaze's partying and vandalism. Then, disguised as an afterthought, Shep says, "I told the boy I was disappointed. He mouths off that he hates me."

"Shit. I'm sorry," Gabe says. "It's just a stage kids go through."

"Out of nowhere. He hates me?" Shep pauses. "Has Oliver ever said that to you?"

Gabe fiddles with the radio, thinks about the two cousins: Blaze a varsity linebacker, loud and insecure long before his parents' divorce; Oliver more like his father, unafraid of solitude, a solid second clarinet in the orchestra and a dependable member of varsity cross country. "Not yet. But he will."

"Yeah? Why's that?"

"Getting older, exerting independence, testing his parents, peer pressure."

"Nothing makes me believe Oliver would ever tell you or Ellen that he hates either one of you. How can you say Blaze's comments are normal?"

Gabe stares out the driver's side window, begging for a car to fly into the pole and end this conversation. "OK. Not exactly normal."

"What is it then?"

"A normal variant."

"I'm trying to have a real conversation," says Shep. "This isn't easy for me."

Gabe softens to Shep's hurt. "It isn't normal, but I wouldn't say it's dangerous either," he says, staring at the pole deep enough to conjure a ripple of suspicion.

.   .   .

"Have I ever given you any reason to hate me?" says Gabe to Oliver.

"When mom drives me to school, she bugs me about girls. Whatever happened to a stress-free drive?"

"Doesn't exist," says Gabe with mock seriousness. The hour is early, but for his body it's late. "Mom's not feeling well."

"What's up with that?"

Gabe realizes that Ellen has successfully quarantined her pain from everyone but him. He lowers the radio to minimize distractions. It's only 7:45 A.M., but he's worried about drunks on the road.

"You're driving like an old lady," says Oliver. He turns up the volume and speeds through the stations. He finds a synthesized tune that sets him grooving shyly.

"I like old ladies," says Gabe. "They made it to old age." The song sounds no different from any other synthetica pounding the airwaves. "You really like this stuff?"

Oliver shrugs, leaks a grin, bobs his head. His son's pleasure in the music kids are expected to like provides a cushioning of the masses, offers Gabe an illusion of safety.

.   .   .

Shep drops in at dinnertime, his habit whenever he works late and misses happy hour at Vincy's. "They're sniffing up my ass," he says, making orgasmic sounds when he finds a beer in the back of the fridge.

"Who?" says Ellen.

"Obviously someone without a clue to your personal hygiene," says Gabe.

"Stan Bigly and his crew."

"What does *he* want?" says Gabe, uncorking his favorite bottle of seven-dollar red. "I've been humping."

"He wants a pole to hang," says Shep.

"That's ridiculous," says Gabe, filling Ellen's glass, then his own.

"Give him one," says Ellen.

Gabe searches his wife's eyes. "You don't believe . . ."

"If it's necessary." Her elbow knocks the cork off the counter. She leans over and stops. Her face knots. Gabe fears any pain that demands such effort to push away. He lays his hand on her back, shows attention and not concern, which would upset her more.

"It isn't easy," says Shep, genuinely flummoxed, not noticing his sister stricken. "I want to deliver."

"Wanting. That's your problem," says Ellen, standing up, proudly holding the cork to her brother's nose. "The necessity isn't there."

.   .   .

A thirty-seven-year-old mother of three, a seventy-two-year-old great grandfather, and a twenty-one-year-old construction worker are all victims of fatal pole attacks during Memorial Day weekend. A thirty-seven-year-old lawyer, a cousin of Stan Bigly, survives his crash. He refuses a breathalyzer on the scene, and a judge denies a court-ordered blood alcohol level. "He's been through enough," says the judge, letting him plead to a misdemeanor charge of refusing a breathalyzer test. "Let him heal."

The holiday weekend is frenzied. Gabe returns home for short naps before being called out again to investigate another scene, another pole. By Monday night he's drained, his patience grinding. "Poles don't kill," he tells the news. "They're the victims."

The day after Memorial Day he's called before Stan Bigly and the State Committee on Automotive Mishaps for 8 A.M. coffee. Nobody stands to let him sit. And when he does, he's fenced in by silence. No offers of misordered coffee are coming.

"How do you explain what happened to my cousin?"

"He's a habitual offender. Four violations for refusing a breathalyzer. He also left the scene after striking a bicyclist."

"Never proven," says Stan Bigly. "He's a good kid. A damn good lawyer."

"Keep him in the courtroom," says Gabe. "And off the road."

Stan Bigly peers over his bifocals

Shep jumps up. "Excuse Gabe. He's busting his balls. He's frustrated, that's all."

Gabe sucks his teeth at Shep, whose protective hand always had the pulse on his sister's welfare. He came through when overeducated Gabe couldn't grovel up a job. Stan Bigly opens his arms to symbolically embrace all the patrons in the coffee shop. "Why would these people, your neighbors, crash into poles?"

Gabe's head rocks from side to side, as if shaking away the question.

"He's overworked," says Shep. "He's not in his right mind."

"Is this true?" says Stan Bigly.

Regardless of how he answers Stan Bigly, Gabe knows he'll leave irreversibly dented.

Gabe scrapes words off his dry tongue. "I can't say what's true anymore."

.   .   .

Gabe stands at the living room window watching Sid and Charlie, now joined by angry others. Some are parents he once chatted up at school events. Their placards show Gabe's face mashed onto a pole body. They're chanting, "Pole lover. Not our brother." They stop when he steps out onto the porch.

"Don't blame me for doing my job," he says.

Someone yells unintelligibly.

"Allow us a quiet breakfast," says Gabe.

Charlie charges up the front stoop. Gabe steps forward to greet him. "Get off my stairs or this becomes a police matter."

"Fuck that," someone yells.

If these are neighbors, Gabe tells himself, then the word needs a new definition.

Gabe identifies true commitment in Charlie's crooked smile, a belief that he owns this moment. Still, he never expects Charlie to actually swing the placard, or miss Gabe's ducked head so badly that momentum jerks his body off the top step, his body a comedic tumble of limbs bouncing down the stairs until his skull strikes the sidewalk with a dull, horrid squish.

After a brief seizure, quiet.

Sid drops beside his son. "Charlie," he says, but does nothing for the bleeding scalp. "The ambulance is coming," says Ellen, rushing out the front door holding one of her good bath towels. Gabe takes it and jumps down to care for Charlie.

"You fucking idiot," Sid yells, standing over Gabe. The crowd moves forward.

Gabe leaves the blood-soaked towel clumped against Charlie's head, scales up to the porch to protect Oliver and Ellen. He can't predict what this crowd will do, but whether it's stampede or serenity, Gabe knows they'll all do it as a group. Blood streams down Charlie's face and cheek. "Put pressure on the wound," says Ellen, lashing out in a loud whisper, but Sid stands there, lost like a child. She rushes to Charlie, kneels in his puddle of blood to staunch the hemorrhaging. "Your boy needs you, Sid."

.   .   .

Protesters fill the sidewalk the next day.

Ellen serves freshly baked oatmeal cookies and coffee.

"What are you doing?" Gabe says, when she returns inside the house.

"They're neighbors," says Ellen. "They're hurting."

"They're protesting against me," Gabe says.

"Don't take it so personally."

"What?" He watches them gathered on the sidewalk, sipping from paper cups. Some yelling, others laughing. He takes her in his arms, lowers his touch to her hips. His love exerts a gentle pressure. "Poles are objects. The poles haven't done anything."

"Then they won't mind." She winces to his focused caress, then gestures outside. "You're worsening their pain."

"By being honest?" he says.

"No, by being selfish."

.   .   .

State lawmakers craft the Party to Economic Prosperity Bill, which allows "intoxicated drivers to operate non-commercial vehicles after demonstrating the requisite proficiency during the Intox," a new part of the standard driving test. Flying through the legislature in a week, the governor signs the bill into law, sipping a pint of stout. Driving at night, Gabe hugs the right lane. He knows safe havens don't exist. A shit-faced driver will always find you, whether you're driving on the road, strolling on the sidewalk, or relaxing in your living room.

.   .   .

Before slipping into bed, Gabe bends to the cracking tune of arthritic knees, bows his head, and prays. Never before has religion played a presence in his life and he doesn't know how to work it. Staring upward and speaking to the clouds feels too easy, and he doesn't believe anything of profound value was ever attained easily.

"Keep Oliver and Ellen safe," Gabe says, maybe louder than necessary. He doesn't explain his absence all these years, make false promises about recommitting his faith, or engage in spiritual bartering. He wants. He's greedy and lazy and maybe even cowardly in his request, but he's desperate too.

.   .   .

The next few days spring offers calm breezes. Gabe finds Ellen stretching, her Breast Cancer 10K shirt drenched with sweat.

"You OK?" he asks.

"Absolutely," she says, "An easy three miles."

Ellen blows him a kiss, as if his skepticism were a flame easily extinguished. "No pain," she says, smacking her hand against her hip. "It feels normal. Beyond normal."

Gabe fears the distorting effect of extremes; when ominous symptoms improve, one can be deceived into believing the new state of things to be better than they are.

"What about the lucency?"

"Probably filled in. Because I feel great." The joy in her face says don't argue. But when he gives her a kiss, he tastes worry.

.   .   .

That night Gabe pleads to the heavy clouds, offers to do anything, absolutely anything, as long as one of the three bodies with bloodied high school jackets isn't his son. The tented hood, the entire front end, is buckled like the beer cans strewn about the car. The face of the driver is embedded into the cracked windshield. Firefighters disarticulate the car from the pole. Gabe breathes violently as each body is examined for what remains of an identity. He calls home. Ellen answers, informs him that Oliver went out to a party. "Anything wrong?" she asks.

He pauses. "Nope," he says, his heart racing. "Just checking in."

"At least those boys took it to that pole," says Shep. "They died on the attack."

Enough anti-pole insanity, Gabe thinks. He hates himself for thinking this, but he doesn't care who these boys are, as long as they're not Oliver.

Then the coroner finds a driver's license in one boy's pocket and waves him over. Gabe's heart contracts to a cube of ice. There's no reason the coroner should need him. He prays. This is the punishment, he believes, for his egocentric and reckless disregard for the boys. "Shep's kid," the coroner says. "Maybe you should tell him."

"Blaze?" says Gabe. Cold shock mixes with relief. His thumb rubs Blaze's photo, insolent even at the DMV. Dead? Beyond the lamplight, at the fringe of the woods, Gabe vomits as quietly as he can, hoping the others didn't notice when he slinks away from the accident scene. Shep charges over. "You're embarrassing yourself."

"I know," says Gabe, a sourness burning the inside of his nostrils.

"You've got to toughen up," he says. "Maybe you aren't cut out for this type of work?"

Gabe gathers himself, slips the license into Shep's palm, silently points to the wreck. He reaches for Shep's shoulder, but gets pushed away. Shep stares at the license for the longest time, wandering over to the pole as if sleepwalking. Then his spine straightens, his fists ball up. He heaves one punch into the pole's body and screams. He swallows, takes a breath, follows with another jab, then a jab and a left cross, jab and cross, until the combination is so fast and furious that Shep misses and falls forward.

"Hold the bastard," Shep yells. "Will someone be kind enough?"

Gabe's expression of dumb disbelief, or so he believes, isn't worn by anyone else. He steps forward, hugs the pole from behind, hands low, ear pressed against the cool wood.

"OK," says Gabe. "Go." He hears bones crack with each blow, feels sweat leap with each grunt, smells blood from fingers swollen like raw sausages. Gabe tightens his hold, comforted by hugging something formidable, that represents exactly what it is. Then he detects gasping from the pole, and a whiff of movement; or believes he does, or wants to believe, begs to believe. A policeman sidles up to Shep. Enough, Gabe thinks. But the policeman offers his black club. Shep grunts as he unclaws his hands to fashion a grip and hacks away as if felling a tree. Wood shards fly. The police, EMS, and the coroner are arranged into a semicircle, offering equal parts space and protection.

Gabe grabs his arm. "Stop, Shep."

"It's not your son, is it?" he says. "It's not your son."

When grief pushes someone to such violence, Gabe wonders, is it still grief?

.   .   .

Sunlight smears the east windows as Gabe sits at the kitchen table with Ellen and Oliver. "War on Poles" cries the headline in the morning paper, a quote from Stan Bigly. Below the fold, a photo of Shep wielding his club with the caption "Justice."

"The doctors kept him?" Gabe asks Ellen, who had spent most of the night in Emergency, trying to calm Shep as doctors tended to the broken bones in his hands. Gabe was busy through the night analyzing the crash scene, thinking about his report.

"A psychotic break," she says, absently rubbing her own hands. "That's what the doctors think."

"Blaze is dead. That's not right," says Oliver, his complexion transparent.

Ellen wipes tears from his eyes. "Your cousin could be an asshole sometimes, but he didn't deserve to die."

"That's not nice," says Oliver. "He's dead."

"Assholes die, too," she says, wiping her eyes with the sleeve of her sweatshirt. "And they die as assholes. Death isn't a road to self-improvement."

"A bone scan is," says Gabe. "Some questions have answers."

Ellen runs the back of her hand over his oily forehead and burning cheek. "I feel great."

"What was it, then?" he asks, not letting her off this easily.

"Hopefully we'll never know." Ellen shrugs. "Even with insurance it's a hell of a lot of money, and that's with both of us working." She pauses. "And we can't count on two incomes, not for the immediate future anyway."

She'd overheard him talking with Stan Bigly, knew about the emergency meeting called for the coffee shop in two hours, the preliminary report expected to be faxed to them in an hour. Shep wouldn't be there to buffer him.

He washes his face, brushes his teeth, and leaves for his office. Trudging to his car, he finds Sid alone on the sidewalk.

"How's Charlie?" says Gabe.

"They don't know. They say prognosis is tricky." Sid pauses. "He'll be OK, I think."

"Tell him I'm sorry."

Sid clears his throat. "It's not your fault."

"I didn't say it was," says Gabe. "But I feel terrible that it happened."

Sid averts his gaze down the street. "It's sad to hear about Blaze. And Shep."

"Thanks," says Gabe, grateful for those simple, true words.

"Will Shep recover?"

Gabe sighs. He wants to give Sid a real answer. "His bones should heal."

Gabe drives stiffly to his office, worried about his first Stan Bigly meeting without Shep. He revisits the pole on Route 6. Apologetically, he rubs his hand over the bludgeoned wood. The grain and shards stained with Shep's blood had already darkened from crimson to a stately maroon; one might conclude it's due to a harsh weather beating. His eye skips from Shep's morning paper photograph stapled into the wood to the targets emblazoned with the words *Aim Here.* But he pauses and considers the blurred photocopy of a missing kitten. Some person found the pole a public service.

At the coffee shop, Stan Bigly and the State Committee on Automotive Mishaps surround two corner tables. A large tea and Gabe's report marks one empty seat.

"Sit," says Stan Bigly, who reads aloud Gabe's conclusion. "Due to the direct impact the vehicle had with the pole, and that the occupants were found dead on scene, one can conclude the pole is the immediate cause of death. If the vehicle had jumped off the road and the pole hadn't been there, it's safe to assume the boys might have incurred minor injuries, but avoided fatal consequences."

"This is a masterpiece," says Stan Bigly.

Gabe settles into his chair, tunes into the din of the coffee shop.

"Shep isn't coming back to work anytime soon," says Stan Bigly, shaking his head. "A shame. The man's a hero. We think you might be ready to take his job on an interim basis?"

The men aren't friendly, but they acknowledge his presence, don't look away.

"What do you say?" says Stan Bigly, his tone impatient with Gabe's silence. "Because we've heard that Jersey barriers are stepping up their attacks."

Gabe takes a sip of green tea, inhales the burnt oils of roasting whole beans, grins to Miles Davis's *Kind of Blue* playing low in the background. He's comfortable at this moment.

8

What's Left Out

"What makes the kidney so special?" asked lawmakers during the Health Transition, before revoking universal coverage for life-saving dialysis. The Midtown Dialysis Center soon went bankrupt, and the new InterCorp Treatment Center bought six recliners at auction and called them asthma chairs. The fates of those patients haunted Dr. Max Reese as he examined the breathless Tamika Sparks; her lips pursing out pennies of air, sweat beading her mocha cheeks, thighs squeaking the same faux leather that once cushioned scarred kidneys. He'd read how the Health Transition was equally unkind to asthmatics. "What makes the lung so special?" thought Max, his white coat suddenly stiff.

.　　.　　.

"Relax, kid," Max said, worry drying his tongue. Two full years had passed since he'd cared for any patient, let alone a patient this sick. "This hallway chair isn't ideal, let's move you to a stretcher in an actual room."

Tamika violently shook her head, unable to fit words into each breath. Suze Mackins, the nurse he'd first met that morning, took her hand. "This *is* the Asthma Room," she said to Max, her bright Irish face blotching with anger.

"Chairs in a hallway?" said Max. "It's an asthma *space*."

"These chairs work well enough for the other docs." Suze shook her reddish-brown hair, then pushed up into the toes of her clogs and whispered heat in his ear.

"Of all the docs in the city, we hire Reese's Pieces."

After two years, the YouTube incident was still chasing him.

"The video left out a lot," he said, grinding his teeth. The ache in his jaw asking why he listened to his dentist, who advised a five-hundred-dollar night guard to prevent his molars from destroying each other when he was asleep. During the day, however, his molars were free to rumble.

"I saw what I saw," said Suze, threading an IV. Max noticed how Tamika didn't flinch when the needle broke skin. Indifference to pain was ominous. He thought about his self-imposed exile from clinical practice, those endless days playing medical advisor for a software start-up strutting the motto "Removing doubt from critical decisions."

.   .   .

The treatment orders for asthma were once swimming in his bloodstream, jumping off his tongue. Bronchodilators. Steroids. IV fluids. Maybe epinephrine. Always oxygen. A stretcher, not a chair. Dredging up each detail now felt like manual labor. He could assume nothing. Tamika wouldn't move to a stretcher. He couldn't even count on that.

.   .   .

"She's nineteen, a lifelong asthmatic," Suze told Max. "Hospitalized twice as a child. Never intubated. She ran out of her inhaler."

The nebulizer hung from Tamika's lips; her head sunsetting between her knees. An inhaler might have prevented this situation, he thought, a simple inhaler.

"Who gave this information?" he asked Suze.

"There's a sister hovering."

Tamika's eyes widened at the mention of her sister.

The empty nebulizer fell from her lips to the tiles. Suze replaced it with an oxygen mask. Tamika pushed the mask to her forehead. "It chokes me."

"You need it," Max said, troubled by the idea of choking oxygen, assault by a savior. He folded his arms. Her stubbornness eluded him. Did it reflect her character, a tough streak that might serve her well in this struggle, or altered thinking from respiratory fatigue? He couldn't distinguish personality from pathology.

.   .   .

Into the Asthma Room stormed Tamika's sister, a planetary force, the heels of her black leather boots bruising the tiles.

"Put that oxygen on your face," she said.

Tamika reared up and quickly obeyed.

"You the doctor?" said the sister.

Max sensed her eyes burning judgment through the laminate of his ID badge. He offered his hand. "Dr. Max Reese."

Her fingernail, painted with a snake coiling around a sword blade, tickled his nose. "Reese's Pieces? Oh, no." She clasped her sister's wrist. "I love you, baby girl."

.   .   .

The video incident was recorded with a cell phone two years before, by another patient, back when he staffed the emergency department at Cityside Hospital. The viral video, "Dr. Reese Falls to Pieces," caught Max arguing with Laslow Birch, uttering the fateful words *get out*. Later, he could watch himself only by pretending that he was somebody else. His voice cut like a whip, one blogger said. The scene ended with Laslow Birch, shirt undone, stumbling into the winter cold. The video left out how Laslow Birch frequented the ED two to three times a day, every day; that he'd sleep, demand food, get discharged, liquor up, and return by EMS to the ED hours later. The video left out Laslow's cursing, his tossing of mashed potatoes. What was left out didn't hold forgiveness for what Max had done. But the truth had teeth, decayed teeth.

Max's resignation letter apologized for embarrassing the hospital. The Cityside General administrators grumbled about Laslow Birch and the many others like him, pulled at their ties and twirled their pens on the mahogany conference table. "Thanks," they said, accepting the envelope. "We can't say you did anything wrong, but there's no way to make it look right." A door in his belly dropped open. Twelve years at the hospital suddenly meant nothing. What started as betrayal grew into paranoia. Max feared that everyone had watched the video—colleagues, patients, the checkout girl at the market, the kids in his daughter's preschool.

.   .   .

"We want another doctor," the sister said, her heavily lined eyes drawn hard as steel.

Max was the only doctor on duty.

"I'll take good care of you, Tamika," he said, the words sticky like syrup. His former therapist said nowadays people suffered little shame from behavior that made them famous. Any choke collar was of his own design.

"This place sucks ass," said the sister, teasing sweat-pasted hairs from Tamika's face. "Poor neighborhoods get doctors other Treatment Centers puke up."

Max didn't reply. He could alter the earth's orbital axis before changing the sister's mind. He found solace in his stethoscope's snug-fitting earpieces, clotting off the sister's remarks while connecting him to Tamika. Her lungs pulsed with unexpected silence. He skipped the stethoscope from side to side. Her wheezing had vanished. Max seized the impulse to celebrate, recalling how this was a trap, the illusion of better, the fatal quiet of airways collapsing.

"We might consider a breathing tube," he explained to Tamika. "You're getting tired. The ventilator will breathe for you until your airways open up."

She pushed herself off the chair, head too heavy for her neck, and teetered down the hallway. "Tamika?" he said. She didn't answer. "Talk to her," Max begged the sister.

"Let's go home," the sister said, clasping her elbow. "Cousin will do you right."

He felt his chest tightening as the sister led Tamika away. His body's outrage against injustice and stupidity. It landed him in trouble with Laslow Birch. "Are you nuts?" Max yelled, looking in all directions for cameras.

.   .   .

"Her choice," said Suze.

"Her choice?" He spread his arms. "She's two breaths short of respiratory arrest."

"Don't let appearances fool you. This is a Treatment Center, not a hospital. She's a customer. The rules are different." Suze turned to Max. He noticed the deep creases around her eyes, regret being held hostage. "I can't lose this job. I've got two preschoolers."

Max understood what she wasn't saying. "Patients are still patients," he said, and chased after Tamika and her sister. Penlight, stethoscope, trauma shears, ID badge, cell phone, keys, wallet rattling in his white coat. He felt like a dropped package.

"Leave us alone," said the sister.

He leaned close enough to smell her gold-plated hoop earrings. "She'll die if you take her out of here."

"She'll die if she stays," the sister said, her jaw cocked in a hopeless smile.

.   .   .

Tamika and her sister turned the corner, walked off into a lost horizon.

"Patients are allowed to make bad decisions," said Suze.

"And when something devastating results from it? I should have forced them to stay," Max said, hands locked on his hips. "I need a coffee. Where can I find coffee in this place?"

.   .   .

Max really wanted control, an identity that didn't wear a dunce cap, a second chance with Tamika. But medicine didn't grant mulligans, and coffee was a desire easily satisfied. When they returned, Tamika sat perched in the row of asthma chairs, her fingers begging him close. "Where did you come from?" he said. The sister's presence cast a shadow like a lunar eclipse.

Tamika settled her head upon his shoulder. Her tears warmed his shirt collar. She gestured to her back. "Rub" she gasped.

"Another neb, please," he said to Suze. Her stylish hair was frizzing now.

Tamika's neck muscles were taut, her shoulders pulled back. "Rub."

Max bit his lip and rubbed. Sweat soaked Tamika's white T-shirt. Through the fabric he caught a tattoo with the script letters JJ and a scar shaped like a knife blade. "You made the smart decision," he said. The sister stepped back as if he was crazy.

.   .   .

The sister whispered into her cell phone, then pumped Tamika's hand with sass and attitude. "Don't worry, honey. Cousin is on his way."

"Dr. Cousin?" Max asked the sister.

"Two jobs plus no insurance doesn't equal doctor."

Cousin appeared without making an entrance, flashing gold teeth beneath a flat-rimmed NY Mets baseball cap. "How's my girl?" He pulled out a stethoscope, a top of the line Litman that Max coveted. Max watched as Cousin examined *his* patient.

"You haven't been using your inhaler?" he said to Tamika.

Tears crept into her eyes.

"No bullshit," he said.

"She ran out," the sister said.

"And whose fault is that?" he lashed at the sister.

Max inwardly cheered as ferocity leaked from the sister's body.

Cousin opened his black leather coat, the inside lining a custom-fitted pharmacy. Max's gaze couldn't expand enough to accommodate the inhalers, pill bottles, and epinephrine pens on display. "She's very sick," said Max. "I need to intubate her."

"She don't need no breathing tube." He laughed. "She needs Cousin." He set his hand on the sister's nape. "And she needs family who has her back."

"What are you? A nurse?" said Max, studying Tamika, jealous of the faith aglow in her eyes.

"Asthma Specialist, Governor Housing Projects."

"Asthma Specialist?"

Cousin pulled out his iPhone, displayed Tamika's records. Max was impressed by the dated progress notes, including lung exam, peak flow, medications, and plan.

"You wrote your own program?" Max said.

"Nah," said Cousin. "A techie in the building who loves his oxycodone."

"Look at her," he said to Cousin. "See the way her belly moves when she breathes in. We call that paradoxical respirations, a sign of respiratory fatigue."

"Feel her pulse," said Cousin. "It's what I call a *don't fuck with me* pulse." He pressed the back of his hand against her damp forehead. "You good?"

She gave a thumbs-up.

"That's my girl. What have you given her?" Cousin asked. Max started presenting the case, then caught himself. "She's *my* patient."

"You're Reese's Pieces."

"If you're so good, how did she get this bad? Why did they have to come here?"

Cousin stepped up into Max's face. "They came on their own," he said, his gold teeth gloating. "I can't force her to fill her meds. Can I?"

Where were the cameras now? Max wondered.

"Don't be a fool." Cousin hissed into Max's ear. "I'm here to help you."

"I'm fine," said Max.

"You need me." Cousin aggressively twirled his stethoscope, then rechecked Tamika's lungs. "She get another epi?"

Max felt his spine turn into rubber. How had he forgotten a second round of epi?

Cousin dug through his coat, expertly injected the needle into her upper arm.

"We'll make things right, Tamika," he said, shooting a look at the sister and Max.

They waited. Max raked his wavy hair. Too many storylines and characters, he thought, for such a straightforward incident. Now he'd permit anything, be open to everything. But Tamika couldn't die. Then her head fell back.

"Tamika," Max cried, pushing Cousin aside.

"She's fine," said Cousin.

"Respiratory arrest is not fine," said Max, fuddling his stethoscope.

. . .

Tamika sat slumped, unarousable. But her pulse was strong, and Max heard air filling her lungs. "She must be exhausted," he said, his heart hammering. He stopped Suze, who had run for the code cart. Suze appeared stricken, devastated by relief. He understood completely.

The sister pressed her cheek against Tamika's lips. "You're all good, baby."

"She might relapse," said Max. "When the meds wear off."

"Uh, uh."

"You must listen to me. I know asthma."

"And I don't? I raised her." She paused, as if to untangle her anger. "Our mother was shot ten years ago, buying a quart of milk at the corner bodega. JoJo died right here. It was Riverside Hospital back then. When they finally let us see her body she had one of those breathing tubes coming out of her mouth and it didn't seem to do her much good." Tears glossed her eyes, then vanished. Never before had Max seen sorrow so ruthlessly beaten down. "I needed my cornflakes," she said.

Disgust riddled Max. He'd never asked Tamika why she feared the stretcher and the breathing tube.

.   .   .

"I don't want her to get worse again."

"That won't happen," said Cousin, updating Tamika's medical record in his phone. "Right?"

The sister nodded.

"How can you be sure?" asked Max.

"This is what I do. Our whole building wheezes. Mold, leaky pipes. Shit, the roaches pay rent."

"Where's the landlord?" said Suze.

"He wants us wheezing," said the sister. "It keeps us from complaining."

"He walks with a cane now," said Cousin, proudly folding his stethoscope inside his leather jacket. "Doing a little complaining himself." He winked at Max.

Suze stood with her hands over her mouth. Max thought she might be sick.

"I never wanted to expand into asthma. The medicinal narcotics industry did me fine. My mom was an ICU nurse. They fired her ass during the Health Transition. I know the guidelines. American Thoracic Society, the British Thoracic Society, whatever. Doctors make a big deal of it, but it's nothing special."

Cousin checked his watch, then led the sister away. "Excuse us for a moment."

.   .   .

Max listened to Tamika's lungs as she slept, measured each breath against his own doubts. She opened her eyes. "You scared us," he said.

"I'm so sorry."

"We should transfer you to our Respiratory Center. We'll observe you overnight."

"I feel good." She rustled in the chair. "Where's sis? This bill is going to break us." She stood, but her body wasn't ready. Max caught her arm, and with Suze's help lowered her into the chair.

"I'll find her," Max insisted. She didn't argue. Max searched the carcass of this former hospital, the empty corridors teeming with absence, with all the sick people forced to suffer elsewhere. He couldn't stop thinking about Tamika.

Her turnaround defied scientific logic; too sudden after the second epi, the reversal too crisp and complete after she'd been clawing for so long. "Consider it a gift," he said, trying to convince himself. Gifts, like tragedies, don't always make sense.

Breathing drew him to an abandoned X-ray suite. He found Cousin with his jeans pooled at his ankles. His hand braced upon the sister's head. Cousin didn't hide his pleasure when their eyes met. "Yes?"

Max cleared his throat. "Tamika wants to leave."

The sister pulled away, but Cousin grabbed her hair without tenderness. He raised his finger, politely requesting that Max hold his thought. Max couldn't believe the sister would willingly submit on her knees in this way. Cousin's back stiffened, his face twisted in unattractive ecstasy. Max turned away. The sister pushed herself off the floor.

"Tamika's all good," Cousin said, breathing heavy, the crisp zip of his fly closing an irrefutable argument. The sister shouldered Max as she passed, knocked him aside. One hand arranged her hair, the other clutched an inhaler.

.   .   .

"What's that look for?" said Cousin to Max as they walked to the dialysis chairs. Everyone had gone, including Suze. Max looked at Cousin, dropped into one of the recliners. He massaged his jaw. "I should thank you."

Cousin sank beside him, groaned. "Damn. These chairs are cruel on the back, would have killed all those kidneys, too, if they weren't already toast." He tapped the armrest. "Asthma Room? Call it what it is. A hallway with chairs. You should see my set up. It's an Asthma Apartment."

"With roaches?"

"I held a lighter to one, the others got the message."

Max pushed his card into Cousin's hand.

"Keep a close eye on Tamika. Call me if she runs into trouble."

Cousin studied the card, seemed to ponder it.

"I know Laslow Birch. I don't think there's a bigger #1 asshole in the neighborhood. His own son won't have anything to do with him."

"Why didn't he speak up when the media was eating me alive?" said Max.

"Laslow might be an asshole. But he was still family." Cousin stood, shaking his head. "Besides, you lost your cool. It's amazing what you can get away with if you don't." He returned the card to Max. "I'm good. We're all good."

9

Empowerment Centers

Patient 0478 sifts through sacks of lethal pills, runs his fingertips along knife handles, swings at the noose hanging from a steel-enforced beam. He nods pleasingly at the many stations in the Suicide Stress Test. Noah sits up, rubs his bloodshot eyes. The patient might actually kill himself. This rarely happens in Noah's work as a Sitter at the East Side Empowerment Center. Thwarting such attempts is the very reason he sits for eight-hour shifts behind a bolted-down metal desk in the locked, soundproof room.

Straining to push back his chair without disturbing Patient 0478, Noah spills the display of Empowerment Center fliers on his desk. The fliers celebrate in flowery cursive the purpose of the Suicide Stress Test, euphemistically called SST. *What better way to test the seriousness of patients' claims to self-harm than to give them the opportunity and the support to end their life?* The cover boasts a glossy photograph of former SST patients, a rainbow of race and ethnicity exploding with smiles as they hold pizza slices weighed down with toppings. The caption: You *can* have it all.

On a good day, a person who is *real,* a true threat to take his or her life, stresses Noah's nerves to the snapping point. This morning it's worse. A sleepless night leaves his body heavy, his head clotted with fatigue and confusion. Lauren left him the night before while he was out with his friend Perk. Gone were her clothes from his bureau and closet, her espresso maker, his radio-alarm clock. Her long pieces for the local newspaper drew notice for their insight and clarity. Noah is baffled she didn't leave him a simple note.

Noah fumbles the fliers into a stack while casting an eye to Patient 0478 as he knocks on the bullet-proof glass of the converted phone booth, steps inside, and touches the revolver welded to a creaking steel arm. Noah resists the urge for alarm. He didn't have time to oil the arm's ball joints this morning. To press the gun barrel to the temple, or inside the mouth, would require great effort.

The paperwork sent with Patient 0478 states he's a recently fired executive. He wears the residue of prosperity: an uncombed mane of salt-and-pepper hair, a wrinkled monogrammed dress shirt that smells of tar and French fries, a flushed face that Noah finds kind and trustworthy. If Patient 0478 doesn't have much to live for, Noah suspects he has much to lose. His excellent health insurance only confirms Noah's security. Studies show people rarely attempt suicide with coverage this good.

Patient 0478 chuckles at the adjustable headrest. He raises his chin. A thoughtful, bemused expression lights his face. He has recognized that this desire to end his life is rash, even silly, Noah thinks, when Patient 0478 pulls the trigger and takes the blast in the chest.

· · ·

While Environmental Services completes a terminal clean on the room and Patient 0478 is carted off to the morgue, Noah sits shell-shocked in his supervisor's office. "This death might qualify as a negligent demise," says Mrs. Curling. Her unemotional gaze peers over stylish tortoiseshell eyeglasses. "Tell me Noah, according to the SST manual, when should a Sitter initiate active intervention?"

Noah holds his answer. He's shaking too much. He's drinking vending machine coffee, which makes him shake more.

"Guideline 2.1: Intervention is indicated once a patient demonstrates commitment to a course of action that will result in imminent harm."

"Yes. Imminent harm," says Mrs. Curling. He has quoted the manual verbatim. In her round face and large gray eyes he sees affection fringed with regret. He would consider her beautiful if not so fearful of her judgment. She reads paperwork Noah filled out twice, the first draft erroneously completed in blue ink, not the official black.

"You're my best Sitter," she sighs. "But if you're found at fault, it will be your second negligent demise. That means grounds for dismissal."

Noah nods from across her desk, muscles cramping, pretending that he isn't fully vested in his 401K in a few weeks. He's exhausted. He can almost convince himself that what happened was a bad dream. The moment plays in his head over and over. The gun flashes. The body flails backward. Noah flinches every time. Shocked. Sickened.

"Do you think you could have prevented this, Noah?

"I don't." His voice trembles under the weight of the words. "I don't know."

· · ·

"I can't believe it happened. I can't believe I let it happen," Noah tells Perk later that evening. They're sitting in an uncomfortably bright bagel shop. "Maybe it's an omen, maybe it's time to call it quits."

"Chill out. Your girlfriend leaves you. A patient kills himself. OK, not a good day. But you get paid to sit. If my trust fund ever dries up, I want your job."

"The job has changed," mumbles Noah, watching Perk eat egg salad on poppy. A mouse scurries out the wall, hugs egg and celery droppings. Appetite gone, Noah finds courage for coffee, careful to sniff the powdered cream before spooning.

"Two years ago, before Empowerment Centers, sitting meant babysitting suicidal or crazy ER patients committed to a psych hospital. They might wait days, even weeks, for a psych bed to open. My job was simple: guard them so they don't hurt themselves or take off. That's it. I was paid by the hour to sit, read, and sketch in my journal. When they created Empowerment Centers to decompress the ERs, I was at the right place at the right time. More money plus bennies. It's a different place now, and a different job."

"Every fairy tale has a fairy and a tail," says Perk, cocking a fiendish brow.

Noah empties sugar packets on the table, fingers designs into the white granules.

"Diego Morales, my first negligent demise, back in the ER days, wasn't really my fault. I was watching three other psych patients, way too many, when the ER turned crazy. A woman in the waiting room hadn't answered whenever they called her name and they later found her sitting in the corner, stone dead. People freaked, and in the chaos, Diego bolted. I never saw anyone run so fast in a johnny and bare feet. The waiting room cheered. A new empty bed. When the ambulance entrance doors opened, Diego turned and smiled at me chasing him. It was a playful smile, not mean or spiteful. But with his eyes turned he never saw the ambulance pulling in."

Perk slams his hand on the table. "That's a bad day," he says. "Lauren and this guy with the hole in his chest, they got what they wanted. Let's get loaded and celebrate."

.   .   .

Noah's nerves are fried circuits the next morning when Patient 0401, a Swallow and Wallow, steps in for her SST. A Swallow and Wallow is someone who ingests or allegedly ingests pills, immediately calls for help, then demands to be left alone. Patient 0401 bathes in the attention from the no-nonsense women surrounding her stretcher: her mother, a sister, and two clinging preschool children. Noah gives the family a sympathetic nod as he leads her into the room and locks the door. To have such an army of love behind you must make the world appear small, or at least masterable.

She rolls her eyes, as if pitying Noah and his job. "My boyfriend is coming."

He points to the sign on the wall. *No family. No friends. Especially no boy-friends or girlfriends.* "For the next hour it's you and . . ." Noah sweeps his hand to display the numerous suicide options. Explanations aren't necessary. Her old records reveal three previous visits, fights with three separate boyfriends, three alleged overdoses.

Patient 0401 is young, narrow-waisted, with suspicious dark eyes and a charcoal-painted mouth. Instead of drinking the charcoal slurry and adsorbing the many pills, she spit it all over the ER staff. Once medically cleared, she was sent to the Empowerment Center for the SST.

Normally Noah isn't so vigilant with Swallow and Wallows, but Mrs. Curling ruled the gunshot blast to the chest a near-negligent demise. She put him on warning, shared with Noah this uncomfortable message from her manager: he was holding onto his job by a pubic hair.

He sits behind his desk, follows Patient 0401's every movement. She appears to wilt while looking around, crushed by the cruel reality of the place. If you truly desire to end your life, the room must feel like Club Med. But if you don't, the mandatory hour in the company of so much opportunity and truth begins to hurt.

"Hector!" she wails.

"The room is soundproof," says Noah. "Focus on why you're here."

"Says who?" she asks. "You? You're no shrink. Maybe a shrink-a-dink."

"How lucky you are," he says, picturing her worried family outside the door.

Mascara tears run down her cheeks. "You don't understand me. Nobody does."

"That's a lot to ask for."

"Fuck you," she says, then settles into the sweet calm, typical of most Swallow and Wallows.

The virtues expected from Sitters as listed in the SST manual—trust, sympathy, and patience—are foreign to Noah at the moment. He sits on his desktop, reminded how Lauren had been a Swallow and Wallow. They had talked as the hour counted down. She believed Noah possessed a penetrating mind. Noah thought the SST cornered people into insight and he was simply a lucky bystander. Perhaps Lauren finally realized this herself and left.

Patient 0401 studies his ID badge, crinkles her nose. "Noah?"

He nods.

She shrugs, shakes her head. "Noah is like a Bible cartoon character. All those animals in a line," she says. "Adam isn't cartoony. Eve isn't cartoony."

"Fifty-three minutes and you can go," Noah says.

She gestures to the room. "Tell me, do you think Noah was a savior, or evil for allowing the rest of the world to drown in the flood?"

"This is only a job," he says. "I'm not saving the world."

"But you're here to save me, aren't you?"

Disarmed by her charcoal smile, Noah can't find an answer.

"You look like that actor, the one who plays all those crazy people. What's his name?"

"Steve Buscemi," says Noah, who shrugs knowingly.

"But you're better looking." She offers her hand. "I'm Maria."

Noah nods, awkwardly holding the compliment. They talk about Hector and her children the rest of the hour, not Genesis. Afterward, she signs off on the discharge packet, which includes a safety contract, a declaration that she will not hurt herself and will seek help if she has the urge to do so; a psychiatric referral for the next day; and a coupon for a free large pizza.

·   ·   ·

Two long days and nights have passed. He no longer believes Lauren will return as inexplicably as she had disappeared. He calls Lauren's parents, her sister, and best friend. They don't answer, don't return his messages.

His head fills with cement. Sleep pulls, but he can't soften enough to go there. He tries the bed, the couch, even the floor. The phone rings. Noah snaps at the phone as if it might fly away. It's not Lauren. It's Patient 0401.

"Hector is shit," she says.

He hears cracks in her voice, silence in unexpected places.

"Why are you calling me?" he asks. "How did you get my number?"

"I thought you cared about me."

"When I'm at work I care," says Noah. "I'm home now," he pauses. "With my own problems."

She hangs up. The caller ID taunts him. Will she do something stupid? He starts dialing, then stops. "She's a Swallow and Wallow, right?" Noah reminds himself. Relax.

·   ·   ·

"Forget Lauren. Call up this Maria Wacko and fuck her brains out," says Perk, pushing his and Noah's empty beer glasses toward the bartender, a beauty they've nicknamed Corset Girl.

"Seriously, Perk," Noah says. His brain floats in beer. It feels good unless he needs to think. "I miss Lauren. I want her back."

"OK. Go get her."

"I can't."

"Why not?"

"I don't know where she is."

"Exactly," says Perk. "Because she doesn't want to be found. She's gone."

"But why? I deserve an explanation."

"Nah. How long were you two together? Six months? You barely accumulated memories with real nourishment."

"We bought stuff. Coffee mugs, towels, even bed sheets. We started a life."

"It was self-preservation. There was no way she was sleeping on your disgusting linen." Perk pinches tobacco from a packet, rolls a cigarette. "She thought you sweet but unambitious, an unfortunate part of her charitable phase." He tells Corset Girl where to set the beers, as if they aren't the only people in the bar at 11 A.M. "Focus on Maria. Fuck her kidneys out. Fuck her until she needs dialysis."

Corset Girl sweeps her raven hair streaked with hot pink off her shoulder, waits for payment with a stiff brow. Perk tips her very well. The hatred in her green eyes softens. Her black leather skirt and a tightly laced corset give the impression of impenetrability. She's too radiant and serious to be tending bar in a dump, Noah thinks.

She allows Perk to smoke at the bar.

"Such a treat," says Perk.

"It's *your* funeral," she says.

Perk snorts at the cigarette now dancing between his fingers. "This is harmless. My DNA is carcinogenic. My dad died of throat cancer. My older brother died of a brain cancer." Dredging tragedy makes him winded. He catches his breath. "When I was a kid, our hamsters grew furry tumors. The Habitrail had a hospice unit. Even my dad's sailboat had a mastectomy."

Cutters slice their skin to kill the pain. Noah thinks Perk uses puns the same way.

Corset Girl is speechless. She restlessly dumps pretzels into shallow bowls.

"My mother died of breast cancer," she says, staring across the room to the St. Pauli Girl poster above the jukebox as she manufactures a smile. "I'm not used to mastectomy being a punchline."

"She needs a hug," Noah whispers to Perk.

"She needs a good . . ." Perk says, thrusting his fist piston-like. He finishes the pint in a long effortless gulp.

"Say something to her," Noah says. "You like her. It's obvious."

"Are you serious? *You* are giving *me* advice on women?"

.   .   .

An earth-shifting quiet fills Noah's one-bedroom apartment that evening. He's reminded of his parents' arguments before they divorced, he and his younger brother listening from the bottom bunk under a tightly drawn blanket. His brother is now bouncing across Eastern Europe on a Fulbright. His parents each remarried several years ago but still busied themselves with the old demons: money, trust, gin.

Noah can't get out of his head. The next few sleepless nights creep by never-ending and when mornings come, they're muddy and difficult to negotiate. He starts arriving early for work. He cleans and oils the revolver, sharpens the knives, secures the noose. He focuses on these details as if they're acts of meditation, only without the calm.

Patient 0430 is muscular and broodingly handsome, the type who appears in bronze light in cologne advertisements. The paperwork states Patient 0430 swallowed pills after his girlfriend broke up with him. "Another one?" Noah thinks, as Patient 0430 uses his piercing light blue eyes to burn Noah into smoke and ash.

"I just oiled the gun," says Noah, meeting his dismissive gaze.

Patient 0430 ruffles his black hair, stares hard at the door. Noah has noticed this tendency before, patients hoping to be rescued by the very people they seek to escape.

"The knives are freshly sharpened," Noah says. Using the anatomical poster on the wall, he traces the path of the jugular vein and carotid artery.

"You know nothing about me," says Patient 0430.

"You told folks you want to kill yourself," Noah says. "If that's so, why should I stop you?"

Patient 0430 grabs a knife, turns to Noah. "You question my seriousness."

"What do you hope to accomplish by taking pills?" Noah says, backpedaling. The blade directed at him can carve through a Thanksgiving turkey, bones and all, and slice breadcrumbs in the stuffing paper-thin. And yet he can't shut up as he falls back into his chair. "Will your girlfriend feel bad for you?" he asks Patient 0430. "Will she now think, 'This person really has his shit together and perhaps I made a horrible mistake in judgment? No, she's going to run as far from you as possible."

Patient 0430's knuckles his eyebrow. "Are you really this stupid, or do you have a death wish?" he says.

"The knife concerns me," says Noah, "But you? Not so much."

The words leap from his mouth, senselessly confident. From the first day of Sitter orientation, they drilled in this mantra: "Don't brush off patient threats." His hand now gropes behind the desk for the panic button. Never before has he needed it, and wonders if it works when no help arrives. Patient 0430 towers close. Noah breathes him in, astonished that someone this good looking can stink so bad, and determines that it might be time for alarm and self-defense.

Then Patient 0430 grins, spins away, and drops to his knees. Noah expects to hear the knife fall, too. But the sharp blade glistens under the man's chin. Noah finds himself silently begging. "Don't do it. Please don't do it. Please." He's scared now, a fear deepened by shame. He's more terrified of losing his job than he was moments before when faced with the threat of losing his life.

"I can't know what you're going through," says Noah, "but it must be painful."

Patient 0430 lifts his head. A critical pause. An opportunity. Noah leaps over the desk with what he imagines is heroic grace, tackles Patient 0430 and kicks the knife away. Saving a life, rescuing someone from harm, heats his blood. He feels molded into the world, even discovers a strange kinship with Patient 0430, a connection cut short when he notices the man's body jackknifed with laughter.

"What's so funny?"

"You're not an athlete, are you?"

Noah finds the knife, pushes it into Patient 0430's hands. "Use it, or move it."

Patient 0430 hums as Noah rushes through the discharge packet. He rips the psych referral slip into the tiniest pieces, waves the pizza coupon as if a winning lottery ticket.

.   .   .

Mrs. Curling calls Noah into her office the next day to discuss Patient 0430's responses to the online satisfaction survey—using a 0 to 5 scale—patients rarely fill out.

My emotional needs were honored: 0.

I was given the time and space to contemplate this difficult time in my life: 0.

Other comments: *The next time I feel like killing myself I'm going into the woods with a rifle and blowing my brains all over the whistling birds and wild-flowers. The people at The East Side Empowerment Center don't deserve the opportunity to save me. I shared the pizza—which didn't suck, but wasn't NY pizza—with my girlfriend and we're now back together. May I suggest a soft drink coupon as well?*

"He's a crackpot," says Noah. "The worse kind of crackpot. He's not genuine."

"The client comes first," says Mrs. Curling.

"Client? Isn't he a patient?"

"You're not a doctor. Neither am I. It doesn't matter. We provide an invaluable service," she says. "What's important for us, right now, is responding to this complaint."

"If he really wants to off himself, send him a list of isolated woodlands."

"We don't want people killing themselves at home. We don't get reimbursed if that happens."

"Most of them are manipulators, attention seekers."

"But we also identify folks with serious mental illness. The SST is about hope. You were glib and disrespectful."

"This guy was never going to kill himself, or me," says Noah.

"How do you know?"

"I just do," he says.

"The hole in Patient 0478's chest argues otherwise." An acid-reflux cringe squeezes her face. "Damn it, Noah. Where's your head when you need it most?"

"You're firing me, aren't you?"

She shuffles papers as if she expects the answer to fall from the sheath.

"I'll be vested in the 401K in a week. Can't you wait seven days?"

.   .   .

Noah trudges up the stairs to his third-floor apartment. The hallway light flickers with each heavy step. Lauren's absence makes his studio feel smaller. The futon couch, the mattress on the floor, the two chairs at the round breakfast table stare at him, dusty and disappointed. Thinking of Patient 0430 makes him disgusted with himself. He rubs his forehead to forcibly expel Lauren from his memory. She left him and he's hurting. Even if she returned now, it would remediate the leaving but wouldn't touch the hurt.

Noah calls Perk, leaves a message on his cell. An hour later he calls again. The urgency to talk to someone is unbearable. What courage it took for Maria to call him, only to be coldly dismissed. Did Patient 0478 expect a gesture from him in the milliseconds before the gun popped? Noah wonders what would have happened if only he had asked, "How are you doing?" A few words might have been enough to allow the trigger urge to speed by. A few fucking words.

Noah walks downtown, hoping to run into a forgotten someone, hoping that something unexpected will happen, which never does when you're wishing for it. He studies the people filling the sidewalks, picks out those who might attempt suicide and those who might actually succeed—an occupational hazard. Depressives can sense other depressives. His depression accounts for his success as a Sitter, which is ironic, since a psychiatric history disqualifies impressive candidates from entering the profession.

Noah visits Corset Girl, asks if she's seen Perk.

"He's spared me lately," she says. She's wearing jeans, a T-shirt, and no makeup. Without her Gothic corset she looks vulnerable, like a turtle without a shell.

The bar is empty, though it's after 11 P.M. and other bars on the strip pulse with live music and the street's a madhouse of horns and hoots.

"He's misunderstood," Noah says, "And he's a quarter of your clientele."

"You're a good friend," she says with a lopsided smile.

"So is he," Noah says.

She throws a coaster on the bar. "What can I get you?"

Noah orders a pint. "So you're an actress-something?" he asks.

"I'm beyond hyphen. I own this pit." She sips too slowly from a glass beneath the bar. "Welcome to my end of the rainbow."

Noah wonders if she's a little drunk as he downs half his beer. He desperately wants to say something kind.

"Do you miss her?" asks Noah. "Your mom?"

"Do you really care?" she asks, pursing her lips with suspicion.

"I care enough to ask the question," he says. "And to listen for the answer."

She takes his glass though he's not finished with his beer. She briefly lifts her head while topping him off. Noah sees a soft light, a glint of promise in her gaze. Later, she doesn't ask him to leave when closing. She locks up, cashes out. She leans heavily on his arm as they walk to his apartment, presses her head against his shoulder. He swells from the thrill of holding someone, the confidence found when counted on for support. Even his sinuses opened up, because when they enter his apartment, he winces from the stagnancy in the air.

Before he can apologize or make excuses, she leaves his arm for the bathroom and runs the shower. He finds an extra towel, puts it to the sniff test, and knocks on the door. Through the dim light he makes out her shadow behind the shower glass. Unsure if it's desire or numbness that drives him, Noah sheds his clothes and stands behind her. He tests her bony shoulders as if her skin might be rigged with electricity, runs his lips over her shoulder-blade tattoo, a butterfly with its bright colors drained from its wings. She leans back. He moves self-consciously. She gently kisses his lips. Mad groping follows, as if they're actors in a bad porn movie, when she pulls away and lets out a scream. He freezes, as if now stuck in a bad horror movie. She jumps from the shower, porcelain skin dripping. She dresses, trips while slipping into her flats, cowers from Noah when he offers his hand.

"What is it? What did I do?" he asks, suddenly sober, still frighteningly aroused. She looks down, screams again, flings open the front door. "I thought you were someone else."

.   .   .

Someone else? Noah wonders, gulping coffee, popping ibuprofen. He's wrung out, wrinkled, and hung over. He needs Ricki Lee Jones at this moment, her first album, or even *Pirates*, her second, but can't find either in his CD stacks. Lucinda Williams is missing. And Tom Waits. John Hiatt, too. Noah can't believe Lauren would take the music he curls up with when the black cloud socks in, the friends he looks to for comfort until he finds his way out.

Too washed out for anger, Noah naps until late afternoon, then shrugs down the block to Hugh's Bruised CDs. He flips through a mess of loosely arranged stacks, stumbling for one replacement. Noah is amazed to find every one he desperately needs. What are the odds, he wonders, feeling the lift of a thin smile. Maybe his luck is changing? He rubs the scratched plastic cases. An unexpected familiarity strikes him. He studies each one, then hangs his head, sick with certainty.

"My ex-girlfriend sold you my CDs without my permission," he tells Hugh.

"What did you do to make her do something like that?"

"Why is this about me?" asks Noah. "Can't she just be insane?"

"It takes two to be crazy," says Hugh. "At least two."

"I lost my job. I just want my CDs back."

Hugh strokes his beard that reaches a belly that Noah hopes is filled with kindness in addition to donuts. Powder streaks his CBGB T-shirt. Noah haggles a price for two CDs. He's grateful to return home with bits of his life he didn't realize were missing.

.   .   .

These tiny reclamations feel like worthy accomplishments. A week goes by, Perk still hasn't returned his calls. Noah's anger shifts to concern when an automated message states his number is out of service. If Perk left town for Harvard Law, he'd believe it. If they found Perk's body in the gutter, he'd believe that too. But he's ashamed by one cruel fact: he doesn't know where to look for him. He never visited Perk's apartment. They always met on neutral ground, shared with each other only what they cared to reveal. When they said goodbye, Noah assumed Perk stumbled back to a similarly lousy apartment with sloping floors, a running toilet, a refrigerator filled with condiments, white bread, peanut butter, and whatever beer was on sale at Safeway. Noah realizes he has no choice but to visit Corset Girl. She isn't a friend, but she's a link.

"Has Perk shown up?" Noah asks, careful to keep an indifferent tone.

She shakes her head. Regardless of who she thought he was a few weeks ago, her eyes sparkle now. He fixes a long, piercing gaze on her. She crosses and uncrosses her arms, tugs on the corset. She finally turns away. He can't figure her out but thinks he's tapped something soulful, fragile, and alluring. She would take her life, if it ever came to that.

"What would you like?" she asks, throwing a coaster on the bar.

"The coaster," says Noah, brandishing the round disc like an Olympic medal and stepping away. Her twisted expression could be mistaken for pleasure or pain. He stops, approaches the bar again. She gasps as Noah snaps her in a headlock and pummels her head with nuggies. His knuckle grates against her scalp. "Are you crazy?" she says, fighting him off.

"How can I be someone else?"

He feels the heat from her nostrils. His touch lightens, until his fingertips comb softly through her thick hair. Her defensive grip on his wrist relaxes. Noah can't tell if she's pushing him away, or guiding him. This intimate confusion lasts only for an instant, when, from behind the bar, she wields a short steel pipe, the grip padded with tape. "Don't you know I can kick your ass?"

"You didn't," he says.

She raises her head, face flushed. "You came back."

Noah kisses her forehead and floats out the bar.

.   .   .

Noah sleeps hard that night. He wakes into a lighter body and spongier world.

He's waiting for Hugh when he opens. "Sorry, dude," says Hugh. "I've got two cats to feed. But I've got a heart. I'll take them from the racks so only you can buy them."

Noah reacquires the first Tracy Chapman CD. He resents paying for things that were rightfully his and stolen away, but he also cherishes them differently than if they were simply pulled off his shelves covered in dust. If only he could find another job, but Sitter skills aren't easily transferable. Each rejection feels like a blow to the back of the head. If not for the treks to the CD shop, he has little reason to dress and step outside.

.   .   .

Finally, he showers, shaves, screws on his best smile, and visits the Empowerment Center to speak with Mrs. Curling. "I heard there were two negligent demises last week alone. Give me another chance?"

She stares off as if fighting a distant glare. "This job isn't good for you," she says.

"But?"

Her raised hand staunches his attempts at denial.

"I know about your depression," she says.

"That's nuts," he says.

"I knew from the moment I met you."

It isn't the depth of the depression, but the open recognition of it that makes him as weak as he's ever felt.

"We can't protect people from themselves. People with serious problems don't start whistling and skipping after a psych visit and a free pizza."

"We're weeding out the low-risk folks."

"Some people are supposed to succeed, right? Why else should the knives be sharpened, the gun cleaned and oiled? Let's be honest, here. Bad outcomes are expected."

"We provide choices, Noah." Mrs. Curling looks away, clears her throat. "Why would you want this job back?"

"It anchors me. Without it, I'm scared I'll disappear."

.   .   .

That afternoon, flopped out on his couch, hypnotized and haunted by *Astral Weeks,* Noah is overcome by a storm of tears, a violent, bone-shaking blow that moves through quickly, leaving him exhausted, emptied, and embarrassed. He wipes his face with the tail of his T-shirt, calls Perk one last time—still out of service. He needs coffee, but shakes a few grinds in an otherwise hollow can. The late sun beats against his window. He changes into a dry shirt scavenged off the floor. Slowly, he collects all the scattered clothes. Then he rips the linen from his bed and yanks mildewed towels from the bathroom. He stuffs it all into a large pillowcase. Hoisted over his shoulder, the dead weight feels like a corpse. But it's only dirty laundry. All it needs is a pocketful of quarters, a few hours, and tiny boxes of soap.

10

Open Ended

Dressed in clogs, hospital greens and a fleece vest, Dr. Jill Gilman descended into her backyard eyesore. A hundred-eighty-square-foot crater, the foundation for an addition to her two-bedroom Cape. She halted construction after they poured the concrete floor, which is where, if she believed what she was seeing, lay a shadow resembling a human body. Nightfall leaned on her tensed shoulders. Hers was a snug dead-end street where yards fit like puzzle pieces. Anyone making camp here, she feared, must be crazy, desperate, or dead. The air turned damp and cool as the steep walls rose above her head, hinting at the pickle of climbing out should the situation scream for escape. She met the darkness with a silver vintage zippo, a strange gift from Robbie after she quit smoking six years before. The flame trembled cautiously toward a sleeping bag massed in the corner. She choked, recognizing the bearded face. "Norm?"

"Quiet, will ya?" Norm Allens yelled, then retreated into sleep-filled mumbling.

She'd last seen Norm two years ago in a trendy market buying four-dollar apples. He'd closed his medical practice and was moving to a Boston condo. Nettie hadn't yet sold their house and vanished with the kids. The state board hadn't yet revoked his medical license. Now, an unlit Coleman lamp guarded his head, and *7 Habits of Highly Effective People* splayed at his side.

"What gives?" said Jill, nudging him in the ribs.

Drool cobwebbed his beard. He pointed over the fence, across the street.

"The Martins live there now," said Jill. "You moved away."

"We have history, don't we? History doesn't move away."

She felt her heart cave. "Come," she said. "I'll make tea. Like the old days."

"Why would you do that? The idea of tea hurts."

"Let's go, Norm. You've caught me on the ass end of a long day."

He grumbled, kicked free of the sleeping bag. She rubbed her eyes. This lumpy version of Norm Allens was a startling change from the fit, middle-aged workaholic he once was. Equally surprising was his nimble clambering up the sidewall, his brawn when pulling her up to ground level, and his steady perch on a bulldozer rut to check back on his sleeping bag, lamp, and knapsack.

"Take them inside," she said.

"Better not," said Norm. "They wouldn't know how to behave."

. . .

"I'm off the grid," said Norm. He slurped tea at the kitchen counter. He wouldn't sit. Rothko barked, sniffed him up like a cavity search.

"Meaning what? Homeless?"

"What was it that Robert Frost said? Home was a place where, when you go there, they have to take you in? So, using Frostian logic . . ."

"Logic?" Jill said, eyes sweeping over his crew sweater and baggy corduroys, his unexpected girth and barrel torso. "I found you sleeping in my backyard. Logic?"

Jill saw struggle in Norm's wind-burned face, thinning hair and gray-streaked beard; dignity in his singular mustache primped like tiny wings.

It had hurt her to read the details in the newspapers. Large payments for enrolling patients in clinical trials. The imposter urine, piss that Norm claimed came from the bladders of actual patients, poured from a stock in his office refrigerator that fit the exact entry criteria for certain trials.

"Why?" she said, leaning against the countertop, arms crossed.

"That's one luxury crater. Private *and* safe."

"I looked up to you."

"The shelter broke me. It's really a sleepover for drunks and druggies."

"Shelter?" she said. "You're a doctor, a smart internist, even principled at one time. When other top internists hightailed it to other states that paid better, you dug your trenches. You stayed."

Norm smiled joylessly. "Virtue. The invisible killer."

"Norm, I'm serving you tea."

"And what? Kindness buys an explanation? Try this. My patients lost jobs, lost insurance, and I still saw them for free—though the liquor stores and drug dealers all got paid. If they had coverage, I wrestled insurance companies for every dime. The news didn't report that, or how I needed a loan to make payroll for my office staff. I hit bottom."

"You hit bottom when you fabricated research."

"I loved medicine. Next to Nettie and the kids, nothing came close. But everyone was playing by different rules."

"That's bullshit."

Norm stared into his tea, contemplative and crestfallen, then gestured to the backyard.

"Why did construction stop? Can't be a lazy contractor. Brad Cutler did our kitchen. He's as reliable as a fresh penny."

"You've been watching?" Jill arched her gaze out the kitchen window. For that instant, the moonlight kissed the backyard and the pebbles glittered like gems. "Robbie suggested an office before moving in. He was going to write a memoir about his relief work. *Slum Dog Doctor* was the working title. We'd reconsider the space later on. Kids room. That sort of thing. Well, discussions on that sort of thing led to fights. He stayed on longer in Somalia, then moved to Haiti and hopped to Liberia. Instead of returning home to break up with me, he's become a serial altruist."

"Maybe he'll surprise you. You can't scrape the bottom of someone so completely that he can't surprise you."

"It took me five years to realize he relates better to populations than actual persons." She sighed. "You in touch with Nettie?"

"Who?" He knocked Rothko off his leg.

She had trained with Nettie, who practiced only briefly before taking a "mommy break." Now she had advertisers flocking to her mommy blog.

"I'll make up the couch," said Jill.

He rinsed his mug in the sink. "I'm an outdoors guy now."

"You can't sleep in that crater," Jill said, thinking on these crazy times, how such words can be spoken with absolute earnestness.

"You calling the police?"

"They'd laugh at me."

"Yes, they would," said Norm, pushing through the door into her backyard.

.   .   .

Making breakfast for Norm the next morning presented challenges. Scrambled eggs seemed too formal, and dried toast felt like dog biscuits. Jill thought one could never go wrong with a classic peanut butter and jelly sandwich. Grape jam. Concord grape. Definitely not exotic flavors, homemade preserves, or specialty jams clothed in jars with fine netting.

She packed the sandwich, apple, and bottled water like a school lunch and took it out to Norm, only to find him gone. Jill kicked the dew-spanked dirt. Not even a good-bye.

.   .   .

At 9 A.M., the clinic waiting room was packed with all the patients scheduled until lunch, plus a few unlucky leftovers from the day before. Jill held her breath against the particulates that thickened the air every morning; the unwashed bodies and greasy McBreakfasts, rotted teeth and gangrenous feet, cigarette smoke and coffee, and the halitosis of hopelessness. She moved through the crowd, head lowered, humming a thoughtless good morning, well aware that it wasn't a good morning for most of them.

A toddler jumped in her path. He smiled with big dark eyes, then slammed her knee with a metal Tonka bulldozer. He giggled, then struck her knee again. Jill grinned with pain, embarrassed that it hurt as much as it did.

"Freddy!" a girl said. He screamed when she pulled the bulldozer from his hand. "I'm sorry," she said, using a ziplock bag dancing with Cheerios to quiet his tantrum. The girl was a teenager, a high schooler. The toddler was two or three. Simple math never made Jill this queasy.

"You've got one cute kid," said Jill.

The chubby teen blew a dark curl from a precociously serious face.

"I'm his cousin. Mom's over there." Mom wore headphones, tapped the tiles with her suede Chuck Taylors. Her lip was split like a baked potato. A tear limped down her cheek.

The shock of Norm Allens's fate reminded Jill that rare was the case anymore when she gave serious attention to how the patients got here, from what cruel height circumstances had dropped them. Recalling an article that described how forcing a smile could instill a feeling of happiness, she wondered if compassion could be similarly fashioned and asked the nurses to push the mother ahead of the others.

Patients protested, jawed on about how the clinic sucks. Jill knew explaining triage to desperate patients often worked like water on a grease fire.

In the exam room, the toddler played quietly with the tongue blade puppets Jill had made. "What happened?" Jill asked the mother, Eva Martinez.

"Eva?" the cousin said. "Talk to the doctor." She looked at Jill. "She didn't want to come. I made her. Her boyfriend beat her up last night."

"Shut up," said Eva.

Eva didn't resist Jill's gestures to examine her, but she didn't cooperate either.

"The ER might be a better place for you," said Jill, thinking domestic violence and a complicated lip laceration were not problems that fit into eight to ten minutes.

The cousin was fighting tears. Jill weighed the teenager's troubled affection, her great efforts to get Eva here, and the probability that Eva will leave if the laceration wasn't fixed now. Eva's record listed a number of missed appointments.

But suturing a lip with a waiting room full of patients? A mess, Jill thought, a mess of her own design.

"This is lidocaine," said Jill. "Your lip will sting, but then it will go numb."

Eva snapped at Jill's hand, and yelled as if under barbarous attack; meanwhile, Freddy amused himself.

Her fiery protests didn't disturb Jill as much as the way Freddy occupied himself, playing as if his mother's screams were Musak to his ears. "Are you and the kid safe at home?" she asked Eva.

"Why wouldn't we be?"

"It must be hard, caring for him and working."

"We're fine," said Eva. Jill heard the beat thumping from her headphones.

"Does dad help out?"

"Dads," said the cousin. "She has three other kids. Freddy lives with her, the others live with my family."

"I'm pregnant," said Eva, her bruised face glowing like Miss America.

"Again?" said the cousin. "You've got to shut that thing down. That's why he hit you, isn't it?" said her cousin. "Last night you told him."

"He was surprised, that's all." Eva Martinez tenderly rubbed her belly. "He loves me."

"Yeah. The others loved you, too."

"You're jealous."

Jill finished suturing, but now Eva was pushing her hand away as she wiped off the dried blood. The wall clock chastised her. What are you doing? Patients are waiting.

"Being a mother, a responsible mother, means more than having babies," said Jill.

Eva jumped off the stretcher. "Yeah?" said Eva. "How many kids you have?"

Jill turned to the computer screen.

"Thought so," said Eva. "And you're how old? Fifty?"

"Thirty-five," said Jill, trying to push a smile and soften her tone. "This wound needs to be checked. Come back tomorrow. And when you do, leave the music home."

Eva darted from the room, leaving Freddy to his Tonka bulldozer and tongue-blade puppets. He whined as the cousin took his hand. Eva slinked back into the doorway, headphones askew on her neck. She held out her hand. "Enough now, Freddy. Come to mama."

·   ·   ·

Jill hustled, missed lunch, but couldn't catch up. She apologized to the six remaining patients who must return the next morning. Frustration followed Jill home. Trolling the backyard, she was disappointed by Norm's absence, though she'd banned him from camping there. These contradictions left her in knots, and she counted on a hot bath to loosen what reasoning couldn't tease apart. She rarely took baths, and slipped stepping into the tub. Rothko scampered through the steam, breathing worry. He jumped up on the tub to lick her nose, then dropped down, licked his own genitals, and traipsed away. She smiled, preferring Robbie's dog to Robbie. She sank into the bathwater, and after a few minutes, found that pocket of perfect warmth, when the phone rang. She closed her eyes, sighed, then got out of the water and answered. What if it was the clinic's answering service fielding a patient's call? But it was Norm, ringing from the police station, arrested for breaking into his old house.

"Maybe you can come down, be what they call a character witness?" he said.

"You need me to vouch for the fact that you're a character?"

"Please, Jill. I have no one else."

She cursed beneath her breath. "How did I get so lucky, Norm?"

Norm's smile, a flash of strong yellow teeth, greeted her. She persuaded the Martins to drop the charges. He hadn't stolen a single thing, and he'd fixed the leaky faucet in the downstairs bathroom. Afterward, they stood outside the police station.

"Let me crash in the crater tonight."

"Forget it. How about my couch?"

They agreed on dinner, at a diner two towns over. Norm feared recognition. Jill couldn't tell him the Martins hadn't recognized the man who once sat across from them at the closing.

.   .   .

The cruel diner brightness exposed his puffed hands, the loose skin hanging from his jaw. She had missed these changes the night before. His odor, sweet and foul, forged a perimeter of empty booths. The waitress left a pot of coffee instead of visiting with refills. Jill ordered grilled cheese and suggested steak and eggs for him, a meal to fill his stomach. Norm shrugged off dinner and picked at a vanilla sundae. "Should I regret what I just did for you?" she finally said.

"I didn't steal anything."

She pushed aside her grilled cheese. "Trespassing. Breaking and entering."

"The Martins never changed the locks. I used a key," he said. "I entered and fixed."

"But I offered you my couch." Jill stared at him, took her first bite of grilled cheese when the waitress slipped the check on the table. "What's the rush? What if he wants dessert?" said Jill.

The waitress pointed her pen at Norm's empty sundae.

"Maybe he wants an entree now. He's eating in reverse," said Jill, disgusted, but finding it hard to blame the waitress. She reached for the check, but Norm snapped it up; polite, but ferociously so. "Norm?" He thumbed a crumble of loose bills, wrinkled and stiff, reminding her of money that had been unknowingly laundered, only Jill couldn't imagine when his clothes had last withstood a wash cycle.

"Leave a tip," he said. "If it makes you feel better."

"It won't make me feel better."

"Then I'll leave the tip." Norm grinned and dumped a pocketful of coins, as well as a silver shank coat button, onto the tabletop.

She felt guilty as they walked in staggered silence to the car. He had fingered the coat button, about to take it back, but kept it there with the smattering of quarters and dimes. She didn't believe leaving the tip was a source of pleasure for Norm as much as an act of hubris, a demonstration that despite his appearance, he understood human etiquette. Jill palmed the button as they left. The waitress would discard it, consider it an insult, though she didn't deserve it, while Norm probably had a coat somewhere with a lonely buttonhole.

"When I was a kid, this strip was hopping," said Norm, stopping before the car and breathing in nostalgia.

The turnpike, two lanes in either direction, was dark except for a car dealership aglow in the distance. An island of promise, Jill wondered, or the final beats of a heart too tired to go on. "The town's bankrupt," said Jill. "No streetlights."

"That's part of it," said Norm. "But it's really about the price of copper. I know folks who steal the copper wire that connects the lamp to the electrical system. They do very well."

"Is that how you got money for dinner?" she asked.

"My first night in the shelter I had my wallet stolen while I was asleep. Now I have a different relationship to my currency."

"OK, no more questions," said Jill, when a man stepped out from behind a bush, faceless in a hoodie. "You have the time?" he said, and leveled a pistol to their chests.

Jill froze, removed her watch. The mugger's hand was thin, and shaking as much as hers. She felt scared, beyond fear; and silly, struck by the inane magical thinking that has sustained her over the years, the belief that her efforts at the clinic bestowed immunity from such crimes.

"I don't have the time," said Norm, "because I don't care about the time."

"Wallet," said the voice urgently. "Phone."

"Look at me. Do you really think I have a phone?" Norm stepped between the gunman and Jill. "Return her watch."

"The watch can be replaced," she insisted.

"Do you want him to have it?" asked Norm.

Jill stood completely still, nervously monitoring the gun barrel as she spoke with Norm. "Under the circumstances I do."

"But if not for the gun, would you choose to gift him the watch?"

"Not really." She nodded apologetically. "Sorry."

"Understood," said the faceless man.

The rest was a blur. Norm slammed the mugger to the asphalt. A tinted Lexus streaked out of nowhere. An explosion of limbs pulled their motionless friend into the backseat, swarmed over Norm for seconds of breathless pain, then sped away before Jill could exhale. Action so quick, motion appeared to stop; violence so pure and hypnotizing that she was blind to her paralysis, until it was too late, and she was flying to his side.

.   .   .

Blood soaked through his sweater. "I'm OK," he said, grimacing.

"Don't move," she said. "I'm calling 911."

"The ER? Are you nuts? I used to sit on the hospital board of directors."

He fought back when she hooked her finger under his right armpit, through a rent in the wool sticky with blood. "Up with the sweater."

"I'm fine," he said. "I've been stabbed before."

The waitress rushed out to tell them she'd called 911.

"Now she helps," said Norm. In that moment of distraction, Jill raised his sweater, enough to view his chest, the shocking three rows of slits on each side. Each slit was protected by veiny flaps fringed with fine hairs. On the right, a flap was slashed, the halves waving helplessly. "What the . . ." said Jill, about to feel sick.

Sirens blared in the distance.

"Please, Jill. I can't go to the ER."

Jill helped him into her car. They headed home in a cloud of unspoken words.

"Thank you," she said, filling the silence. "For defending me."

"What you saw on my chest," he said. "I think they're gills. I'm growing gills."

"Sure," said Jill, as if she'd seen this before. "Why not?"

"Because I have lungs. This isn't normal aging. Arthritic joints, embarrassing hairs sticking out your ears."

"No it's not, Norm. Shit. You have entirely new anatomy. You could have told me."

"The 'gill talk' isn't easy to slip into conversation," he said. "Besides, why should I confide this information to you? You've got serious issues yourself. Stopping construction and doing nothing with that crater. And it's been months. That's not normal. What's up with *that?*"

She nosed into the driveway. The engine died knocking. They remained in the front seat.

She saw Rothko jumping in the living room window. "You had no right to spy on me."

"I have gills," said Norm. "I operate under different rules of etiquette."

"The gills defense," she said, swimming in confusion. She could accept this absurd counterargument and believe it as valid as any philosophy or jurisprudence.

They stepped out of the car into evening's damp chill. He hugged his sleeping bag, threw the beaten knapsack over his shoulder.

"I could dress that wound."

"I know."

"I *should* dress that wound." She flipped him the silver coat button. "I'm sorry. I just stood there during the attack."

He nodded, creaked the hinges on her backyard gate. "Don't feel so bad. I wasn't defending you. I was defending the moment."

He dug into his pocket, wincing as he moved, and propped her watch on the fence post.

.   .   .

When Eva Martinez didn't show for her follow-up visit the next day, Jill felt wronged, even duped, caring for someone more than she cared for herself. She called twice, expressed cheap concern to a disembodied voice that may, or may not, be Eva's voicemail. She had many patients from this neighborhood where crack and alcohol could be found on every street corner, while fresh fruit required a bus ride with a transfer. But when clinic was over, she went in search of her.

The front door bearing Eva Martinez's address was a striking indigo, a splash of hope against a porch with rusted rails and gimped folding chairs. Jill knocked lightly at first, then leaned in with a clenched fist. The door cracked. Inside the frame braced a dark, handsome man with slick black hair and a coiled charm.

"Is Eva home? I'm Dr. Gilman." She raised her stethoscope, as if waving a white flag or a string of garlic. His invitation was a backward step. "I'll wait here," she said, trying to tame her heartbeat from knocking against her throat. But wasn't that why she came here, and didn't wait for Eva to come to clinic, which her colleagues thought more prudent. The clinic provided security, the comfort of easy opinions. Jill needed this fear, which contained within it the promise of kindness.

Eva joined her on the cement porch. Her lip was healing. Make-up shaded a bruised eye.

"You didn't have that yesterday." Jill reached out to examine her, but Eva snapped back. The young man stood in the doorway. Eva nodded. The door slowly shut.

"You were supposed to come back today for a wound check."

Eva thumbed the front pockets of her jeans. "I know I'm bruised. I don't need you to tell me that."

"There's a risk for infection. And you're pregnant. A young mother." Jill was aware of the curtain shuddering inside the window, and Eva pretending not to notice.

"A bad mother, right? I could tell you had some sort of problem with me."

Jill narrowed her eyes. "I moved you ahead of the others."

"I didn't ask for no favors."

"You weren't appreciative," said Jill, biting her trembling lip. "I fell behind because of all the time spent with you. Several patients had to come back the next day."

"Yeah? Well—" Eva's big eyes turned to the gray moon peering over the rooftops. "I'm sorry about that."

Jill felt her impressions listing. She studied Eva's face.

"How's Freddy?"

Eva chewed on a thumbnail. "None of your business."

.   .   .

Jill returned home cursing herself, lost in the trappings of her selfish concern. Patients missed appointments all the time, and she didn't visit them at home. She sought calm, or the promise of a smoother anxiety, in the paradoxical form of Robbie's sweatshirt. Years had softened the heavy cotton, washed out the Penn Crew lettering. Hanging almost to her knees, the sleeves sagging beyond her fingertips, it swaddled her in a forgiving warmth and conjured memories so sweet she could taste them.

She headed to the backyard. Norm was snoring. She slid into the crater, the soil and pebbles cutting into her skin beneath the sweatshirt. Jill sat cross-legged, her sweatpants useless against the chilled cement. Norm appeared well tucked, the sleeping bag zipped to his chin.

"We need to do something about this, Norm. It makes me uncomfortable."

"You're uncomfortable? Try sleeping here."

"Unfair. I've asked you inside. How many times?"

Norm turned away.

"It's not the easiest adjustment," he said.

In his glowing disgrace, his pure and transcendent decay, she saw a person she didn't know she needed. Someone who had lost the luxury of judgment.

"I told a patient, a young mom with kids, now beaten up and knocked up by her boyfriend, that she was an irresponsible mother." Jill held her breath. She couldn't tell if he was listening or sleeping. "I told her that being a mother means more than having babies."

"You're entitled to your opinions."

"Some of us want to have a family. Badly. But we try to be responsible about it."

"What counts as responsible behavior?" said Norm. "And who counts it?"

Jill felt her face drop. Listening to the stories of those who suffer was the hardest part of her work, but it paled with sharing her story with someone who had suffered more.

"The girl wants to be loved," he said, in a surprising, solemn tone. "If anything, maybe she's an irresponsible love seeker."

Jill shivered.

"Start over elsewhere," he said. "You bought this place in residency. It's a tiny Cape. That's all it can be. An addition would make it a tiny Cape with an unsightly growth."

Norm turned to her. His face creased into patches of pride and disgust. "Drug company hardball did me in. Someone in my office reported how I didn't follow study protocols. Whether patients were assigned to placebo or the study drug, I still gave them the standard of care."

"You were a double agent?" said Jill.

"I put my patients first."

"By polluting research?"

"Treatment was of the highest caliber. Pharmaceutical money kept my practice alive. That's all I cared about. This cost shifting felt so right, even when the lawyers told us to put the house, cars, and investments in Nettie's name. I never expected to be punished. I never expected that one day Nettie would take the kids and move home to Kansas City."

She reached for a response. Her mouth hung open in painful silence. She felt his pity, which hurt worse.

Norm sat up. "I have no regrets," he said. "Look at me, what's become of me, and yet I regret nothing."

Tears filled her eyes. "Let me check that stab wound."

"Don't take this so personally," he said. "It doesn't matter."

"Please?"

Norm pulled off his sweater. His sleeves were stuffed with balls of newspaper, hiding rounded arm nubbins below the elbows. Was it possible she hadn't noticed the previous night, or made assumptions from his expert use of a long sundae spoon? She would consider this all a hallucination if not for the knife wound, now pus encrusted and angry red.

"It's infected," said Jill, her body quaking. She tried to control it by sounding clinical, by finding protection in that which was familiar and understood.

He emerged from the sleeping bag, stretched out, belly up. "I want you to feel my chest, just feel it. If you can do that, go crazy with the infected gill."

Her trembling fingertips skimmed rubbery skin, explored the serrated ridges and filamentous hairs. "They're real," she said, disgusted and amazed.

"What? You think I'd get gill implants?"

"Thinking isn't much help at the moment." She filled her lungs as if each breath might prove to be her last. This unsettling notion was followed by a more disturbing thought. This makeshift species resembling a junkyard sea lion might have had its origins in honor.

"This has to be our secret," said Norm.

She wobbled when pushing up to stand. "I'll get you Tylenol."

She collected a flashlight and supplies from the house. Her head dropped when she returned to find Norm in a deep snooze. How can heavy sleepers survive in the wild? Tending to his infected wound, she was startled to find the water bubbling, the gills quivering hungrily. She laid wet towels over his chest. She dressed the infected area with gauze. His spiny skin wasn't receptive to tape, and she was certain the dressing would fall off in the water. But she kept at it. Down here, one foot below the frost line, doctoring felt undeniably right, and she didn't want this feeling to end. For hours she sat with her fingertips tickled by the grateful puckering from beneath the towels. Her peace interrupted only by a disturbing thought. What if there were others like Norm? She dismissed that idea, while at the same time reaching beneath her sweatshirt and running her hand over each of her ribs.

Daybreak pink smeared the sky. When Jill opened two cans of tuna, Norm bolted upright. She took strange pleasure in how Norm licked the cans clean, then rubbed his face in the dirt.

"I once took Nettie for scuba diving lessons in the Keys," he said. "I couldn't do it. The air hunger got to me. Now, Key West here I come."

"I've decided to ask Brad Cutler to fill in this hole."

His once dandy mustache slumped.

"What will you put here?"

"I'll start with level ground. That will be an improvement."

"Really?"

"I thought you'd be happy for me," she said. "I'll give you a lift somewhere. The Keys is a reach, but the cove is nearby."

"That's always the case. People say they want to help, but only on their terms."

.   .   .

The next day Norm was gone. She reported a missing person to the police, but hung up when they asked where he was missing from. Besides, she couldn't say what he needed, and what response was called for. She called Brad Cutler, and he came around in his pickup in the early evening. "About time. Let's make things right."

Jill hesitated.

Cutler ripped off his baseball cap. "You're not changing your mind?"

She nervously talked about Norm.

"Norm's killing business," said Cutler, his boot kicking up dirt.

"Norm's been elsewhere?" Jill asked, feeling spurned and betrayed.

Cutler pointed in several directions.

"You're not disturbed by it?"

Brad Cutler coughed, smacked a pack of cigarettes. "Not anymore."

His men came around Saturday. The bulldozers and backhoes replaced the soil, but couldn't fill the hollow whistling through her. She took Rothko for a walk along the cove. Rothko sprang forward and bounded down the rocks, leaping into the low tide, barking fitfully. "Get back here, Rothko," she yelled, worried for the baby geese innocently resting in the tall grass. Then, gauze bobbed toward shore like a bloody raft. Jill jumped down, shielded her eyes. Her heart danced as she looked out. Sunlight sparkled off the water. The winds were calm, the unsuspecting sailboats lounging with uneventful grace.

11

Avignon

The concierge at the Paris hostel threw him out the very day he arrived. He was now on a lurching train from Paris to Avignon, folded inside a hangover, the last drop of wine finally wrenched from his stomach. His blistered tongue tasted of bile and humiliation. He was rethinking his decision to visit Europe. Maybe he wasn't the type of person who leaves school to see the world? Maybe he was the type of person who dreams about leaving school to see the world but never leaves?

He never planned to visit Avignon, though many tourists considered it a vacation destination. A week earlier, before landing at Charles de Gaulle, he had ripped apart his stiff and glossy *Lonely Planet* to lighten his backpack and kept only those pages dealing with the cities on his itinerary; his diligently outlined enemy to wanderlust. He didn't know about the Palace of the Popes, the Musée Calvet, or the Saint-Bénézet Bridge, but even if he did, he wasn't up to visiting any sites.

Matters would have ended differently, maybe even amicably, he believed, if he could have communicated with the concierge in French. He was a monolingual person who believed great power came with speaking another language. In high school he studied French without success. The trip to Paris was in part an experiment in immersion, a quest for lost knowledge. He was a different person now and believed he'd engage with the language differently.

During his first week in Paris, the French people who understood his caveman French spoke English, too. They didn't furrow their brows when he slipped English words with a French accent into conversation, allowing him incremental liberties until he was speaking gleefully in English.

The concierge didn't understand any English.

The previous day began with a frustrating argument over change for postcards with a street vender on Boulevard Saint-Germain. His French/English dictionary proved futile. Unexpected relief came from two Mormons walking by. These affable and polite young men had been in Africa doing missionary work and were spending the summer in Europe before returning home to Idaho. They spoke French effortlessly, the way they wore their backpacks and the crew-neck sweaters knotted casually around their waists.

He insisted on buying the two Mormons beer or a café au lait. They refused. No alcohol. No caffeine. Instead, they took him to an ice cream shop on Île Saint-Louis, where the line stretched into the cobble-stoned street. The tiny, velvety rich scoops loved his mouth profoundly. It tasted so good he wanted to cry.

Until that moment he'd been considering calling short the month-long trip and returning home. He'd had enough museums and cathedrals. He was overdosing on omelets and jambon fromage, cheap meals with French names easily remembered. He wrote voluminously in his journal; impressions of sites like the Louvre—Grand Central Station with art—and the flamboyant and vulnerable Pompidou with its guts on the outside. He wrote about failing at fun. If he wasn't having fun, he should be back home in school, where not having fun had a greater purpose.

The Mormons were on their way to a hostel they knew about. They learned he was traveling by himself, asked if he wanted to split the price of a room. They took charge and checked in. The three of them dumped their backpacks in a room with two bunk beds, washed up and went for breakfast. He lavished in their company, felt emboldened by their fluency and innate knowledge of the City of Light. He felt less like a reticent, awkward tourist and more like a traveler in search of adventure. By late afternoon, however, he quickly tired of their endless tales of daring and sacrifice, and wondered if they considered *him* someone in need of saving.

Professing the need for a bathroom, he darted into a café and threw back an espresso. He drank too fast and burned his tongue. He chugged a cold beer to numb the painful blister and rejoined them on the sidewalk. They removed their sunglasses. He sensed their disappointment. He didn't consider himself someone the Mormon people should be disappointed with. Needing to break away from their judgment, he lied about a prior dinner engagement that evening. He didn't think he was the type of person who spoke of "dinner engagements." Plans were made for breakfast the next morning. They parted with indifferent handshakes.

He ate standing beside an outdoor crepe vendor, blissfully alone, when a stocky guy wearing a stars-and-stripes bandanna on his head ordered a "crape." A wine bottle poked out the top of his backpack. Wine made them fast buddies. His new buddy showed him how to smack the base of a wine bottle to pop the cork without a corkscrew. Two bottles later he was brave enough to try it and nearly broke his hand. The buddy, wheezing with laughter, checked his watch and froze. "Shit. I'm late for my train. Let's go."

"Where?"

"Amsterdam. Let's take this party on the road."

Was he the type of person who suddenly leaves Paris for Amsterdam, a city not on his itinerary, with someone he'd just met, who might be part of a vicious band of thieves? Could he coldly walk out on the Mormons? His newfound buddy kept pointing to his watch, his face bright and lively, eyebrows arched like opening gates.

Yes, he *was* the type of person who leaves Paris for Amsterdam at night, the type of person who sneaks out on kind people who befriended him. Strangely, this unseemly side of himself felt great. He wasn't thinking about what he should do. The spirit of companionship, if not real friendship, and the wine-induced courage made him feel substantial and rooted in the moment.

They ran to his hostel to pick up his backpack. His buddy paced the sidewalk while he bounded upstairs to his room. The door was locked. He didn't have a key. He found the concierge in her apartment downstairs. She refused to open his door. The Mormons had secured the room earlier in their perfect French. She didn't recognize him, never saw him enter or leave. His slurred scraps of French words couldn't make his crazy begging comprehensible. Nobody was around to translate. He stumbled backward when she slammed the door.

He never decided to charge upstairs, two at a time, or to ram the door with his shoulder. He was surprised the lock snapped so easily from the jamb. He grabbed his backpack. His buddy now stood in the doorway, choking with laughter. He saw himself swell in his buddy's bloodshot eyes. Irresponsibility and vandalism were such easy achievements. He wanted to leave the Mormons a note. Searching for a spot where it wouldn't be missed, he realized the backpacks beside the beds weren't theirs.

The Mormons had left *him*. Two men who had devoted years to tribes in inner Africa abandoned him after half a day. He swallowed the hurt and with his new friend careened to the Metro and the Gare du Nord. The pang sharpened when they arrived to an empty platform, the train to Amsterdam long gone. "Fuck!" his buddy screamed. Using drunk logic, he reasoned that they should return to his hostel and set out for Amsterdam in the morning. Hadn't he already paid for a room?

The concierge confronted him immediately. She yelled, threatened him with a large wooden spoon. His buzz and his confidence evaporated. He confessed, disgusted by what he'd done. Aware again of his blistered tongue, he lisped how this was not him. He was not someone who gets drunk and breaks locks.

An impishly grinning girl from Austin translated with a Texas accent. He could tell she thought this entire scene silly. He knew he'd be one of the many stories she'd tell after returning home. The concierge demanded that he pay for the lock and leave immediately. He shook his head. He'd pay for the lock only if she let him stay the night. The girl from Texas nodded, impressed. The concierge conceded.

He planned to sneak his buddy into the room, but the stranger had vanished. He couldn't remember his name, if he'd known it at all. Physical details blurred as he vomited through the night. He began questioning what had happened. Did it belong to memory, imagination, or was it part of a greater confusion?

The hangover clamped into his skull with slowly tightening screws. He left the hostel while everyone was asleep. Wearing sunglasses, he trudged to the Metro toward the Gare de Lyon. He held a month-long train pass. He picked a city almost three hours away, long enough for a nap. That's how he came to be in Avignon, a medieval city on the Rhone River, on a blustery Sunday morning when many shops and banks were closed. The sky was a sheet of oppressive blue. A nearby bank machine wouldn't accept his card.

He'd spent most of his cash on wine and the lock. There was enough left for a café au lait and a croissant. He sat at a small round outdoor table, under a large umbrella that shielded his eyes from knifing sunlight. He couldn't believe everything that had happened yesterday. He was embarrassed and impressed by behavior that was destructive and rebellious, and hoped that, like the hangover, it would disappear.

The first sip of coffee served as a reminder of his burnt tongue, but the taste filled him with promise. He stretched his body in the chair, took a slow grateful slurp before a gust of wind lifted the umbrella and brought the table, coffee cup, and croissant crashing down. He surveyed the damage, too broken and sick of himself for anger. He considered the cobblestones at his feet: was he the type of person who eats food off stone harboring centuries of filth? Does the five-second rule apply here?

He wiped the croissant on his jeans and ate as he walked. Regardless of how he adjusted his backpack, it felt awkward on his shoulders. He found a park with an empty bench. Shutting his eyes intensified the pounding in his head. Slowly, sleep began to lift him, when bird guano splattered his denim jacket. His eyes flew open. He never considered himself someone birds shit on while sleeping off a hangover. Hoisting his backpack, he dragged himself back toward the train station. He wasn't religious, but thinking of this incident as divine punishment brought him a measure of solace.

He cleaned his jacket in a public restroom. The man shaving at the sink next to him pointed out gray globs in his hair. The man looked like a street person, or at the very least, someone down on his luck; baggy slacks, suspenders off shoulders, oblivious to people waiting to use the sink.

He wondered about himself. Did he strike others as someone who might bathe at the sink of a busy public restroom? He splashed his face. Soon his head was angled under the faucet, his hands cupped to rinse the shampoo from his hair. It felt good, the cool water, the clean smell of soap, the fresh-scrubbed tingle. Restless whispers lined up behind him, but he heard the comb sliding through his slick hair, the screws loosening in his skull.

"Merci," he said, smiling, pushing his last euro through the soapy counter toward the other man, who gave a nod. No other words were spoken, and yet he believed they had understood one another completely.

A few hours later he was back on a rocking train. He was ready to leave France. Maybe he'd cross the Channel into England. With language less of an obstacle, it might be easier to become the type of person he was capable of being if he would only stop thinking about it. His breath fogged the window as his eyes wandered over the endless fields, timeless in the late afternoon sun, and settled on a herd of grazing cows. He watched how they chewed, their idle contentment, and glimpsed the type of person he really was: the type of person who yearns to be somewhere other than where he is.

12

Fortunata

Lawrence Wellbourne, CEO of Poultice Pharmaceuticals, announced to a roomful of vice presidents the ominous news: they didn't have any new drugs in the pipeline—now, or in the near future. "Our position on Wall Street will soon be doggy style," said Wellbourne. "There will be cuts, obviously. The cuts will hurt. I'll hurt." He nodded wistfully. "Sometimes bad things happen to good people."

Simon Dunn's chest fluttered as he watched colleagues curse and sink into their seats. Simon wanted to ease their worries. Hadn't they all been in this precarious place before? Didn't they survive and even thrive as a result? Simon grabbed at his heart, nervously padded the front of his wrinkled suit jacket. His inside pocket was buzzing. Relief blossomed into excitement when Sydney's name lit up his cell phone. He excused himself, ignored the gauntlet of disbelieving stares as he pushed his tall, hulking frame through the door. They expected him to say something, not leave the room. But his daughter was calling from college.

"Not at all," he said to Sydney, who was sobbing. "It's a perfect time."

Two long weeks had passed since Simon returned her to campus after winter break. Sydney cursed the heavy traffic while he celebrated the extra time with her, secretly coveting roadwork and broken-down vehicles. Her tear-soaked voice now provoked fresh longing. He waited, confident he would pull out the right words, the unexpected joke, to make her feel better. Then she launched into revelations learned in a medical ethics course: landmark abuses of human subjects in clinical research—Nazi Germany, Tuskegee, Willowbrook.

Blood pounded his temples.

"And recent creepy third-world AIDS research. Poor, uneducated people were given either a study drug or a sugar pill," she said. "But did they give *informed* consent? Did they know there was a good chance they'd receive a dummy pill and die?"

Simon loosened his shirt collar, pulled at his tie.

"Did they understand they were subjects in a drug trial? That the white coats were researchers testing a drug, and *not* doctors there to take care of them?"

"How should I know?"

"Poultice ran some of the most notorious clinical trials. You were involved. You! Simon Dunn, Director of Clinical Applications and Public Information. My father."

"It's very complicated," said Simon.

"I thought I knew about your work. But you have a secret life. You're a Nazi."

"Nazi? Half the people were given state-of-the-art drugs. If not for the trials, they would have received zero treatment."

"And the other half?"

"We gave them a dose of hope. They were left no worse. Status quo."

"Their quo. Inadequate quo. Poverty quo."

"Listen, baby," he said. "You were told only one side of the story."

"You, your company, and the Nazis: all lumped together."

"Are you done?" Simon thumbed his eyes hard. The silence rippled. "Anything else on your mind?"

"Well, could you spot me some cash until next week?"

"How much of my tainted money do you need?"

.   .   .

"Sydney called me a Nazi," Simon complained to Autumn as he cooked a breakfast to nourish his wife out of her recent depression: cheddar, mushroom, and onion omelets; sliced melon; and plenty of black coffee.

Autumn hunched over the morning paper, absorbed in what she was reading, sipping from a Poultice coffee mug bearing their motto *One step ahead.*

"She'll grow out of it, honey,"

"She's twenty. She's grown," said Simon.

"Nineteen. But you're right. Maybe she won't."

Autumn finished the article, slapped the headline. *Honor student slain outside high school.* "Trevor Jones. The kid's captain of the basketball team. Big Brother volunteer to some kid even poorer than he is. Police think the bullets were intended for a drug dealer nearby." She pushed back her chair. "Argh." Her groan exceeded her normal outrage. Simon blamed the lack of funding and doomed fate of Kids Now, the nonprofit she directed, providing services to families and children who are sicker and more deprived than any kid deserves to be.

"What should I do about Sydney?" Simon asked. "And her skewed view of my work."

Autumn tossed her stylish black-framed reading glasses onto the table and ran bitten fingernails through short, silver-streaked black hair. She sank her teeth into a wedge of melon. "Why do bad things always happen to good people?" she asked.

Her sympathetic, world-weary tone warmed him. He bent and kissed her. She responded with hesitant, preoccupied lips. He realized she'd been referring to Trevor Jones, a stranger, a dead stranger. He examined the boy's photograph. The sight of his handsome face concentrated the tragedy. Instead of another headline he turned into someone's son. Simon pushed the omelet aside, though impressed with how good it turned out.

"A bullet scratched the drug dealer's ear. A scratch!" Autumn closed the newspaper. "I mean it. Why do bad things always happen to good people?"

"That Trevor did some good things doesn't necessarily mean he was a good person. What were his intentions? What if he did those things to buff up his . . ."

"His what? His obituary? He did these things to have a kick-ass obit?"

Simon felt off-balance. The appropriate words eluded him, the wrong ones kept coming. "I'm saying he *could* have had a dark side. Even people we're close to remain, at some level, incompletely penetrated. Sometimes bad things happen to bad people."

"A young person died," said Autumn. "Is that ever good?"

"The south side of the city is a tough place," said Simon. "People die."

"Did you really just say that?" Autumn asked, standing slowly. "You did."

"C'mon. Sit down," Simon said, wishing he could state the truth without an accent of condescension.

Autumn swooped up her beaten leather brief case. Simon knew she was headed to the office of Kids Now, a former barbershop with three swivel chairs on which kids loved to ride up and down, a wall length mirror, and a sign on the wall that might explain why one business, and now a second, had failed. *All haircuts $10, except long hair.*

Simon worried about her as she drove off in her fifteen-year-old Subaru, not the coltish BMW he had bought for her fiftieth birthday three years earlier. "If bad things really happen to good people," he wondered, "Autumn was a walking bull's eye."

· · ·

Simon was accustomed to waiting in airport security lines. He stood in his socks, big toe curling through a hole. He patiently held his wingtips, belt, and laptop, at peace with the delays. He traveled often to speak on behalf of Poultice Pharmaceuticals. The best part was watching the audience's bright-eyed anticipation as he was introduced, his personal accomplishments at Poultice listed, his seventeen years of employment noted. His longevity, he believed, attested to his character. His personal investment in Poultice's mission earned him the audience's immediate attention, if not full-blown respect.

Wellbourne's announcement chilled him more than he cared to admit. What if he was fired, or laid off? There were rumors. "We need to become leaner, more efficient, at all levels," said Wellbourne at a recent manager's meeting. Money wasn't the issue. Simon had saved, invested wisely in his 401K. But if he wasn't a Poultice executive, would any audience care about what he had to say? Apart from Poultice, who was he?

.   .   .

"Omelets again?" Autumn said, sitting at the butcher-block island, her hands cupping a glass of bourbon as if it harbored a warm fire. Simon beat the eggs, nodding. His cooking expertise was limited. "Take off your ski jacket," he said. "Stay awhile."

"You should've seen her lying there, a sweet little girl connected to all these tubes, fighting for her life."

"Don't blame me for Maria Sanchez. We don't even make asthma meds."

Autumn had told him the story repeatedly. Cute six-year-old with severe asthma; family forced to choose between medications, food, rent, and electricity.

Kids Now had helped pay for Maria's inhalers in the past, even arranged for a pro bono lawyer to pressure the Sanchez's landlord to fix the mold and leaky pipes. The landlord agreed but never did a thing, and threatened to evict the family—husband, wife, and three children—if they pushed the issue.

Autumn drained the glass, smacked her lips, and went upstairs.

Simon found her leaning on the wrought-iron balcony outside their bedroom, pensively looking out onto the backyard she designed around a peaceful Japanese garden.

"Winter has no business in March," he said. Moonlight cut dreamy scars into the frozen pond, cast a mournful glow on a garden that for now was growing only sand and stone. "You did what you could," said Simon, holding her from behind.

"It wasn't enough," she said. Her back muscles stiffened to his touch.

"That's the paradox of enough," said Simon. "There's never enough of it."

.   .   .

Maria Sanchez recovered, and Autumn footed the bill for her next month's medications without telling the family Kids Now was broke.

"What happens when these meds run out?" asked Simon. "What about the next kid who needs meds? Where do you draw the line?"

"She's going back to the same lousy environment that put her in the hospital."

"Talk with Dick Levy. Accept the grant. It will stop the bleeding."

Dick Levy was VP of Charitable Gestures at Poultice. Despite the anticipated slash in profits, he had offered to float Kids Now for the next year.

"I won't accept money from Levy and Poultice," said Autumn. "People will think I'm in the pocket of the Big Bad Wolf."

"Nobody has to know."

"I'll know," she said.

"Is it about you, or the kids?"

"Stealing from the rich to give to the poor is still stealing."

"But we're *giving* you the money."

"You're still the Big Bad Wolf."

.   .   .

While Simon waited for the green light, he fingered through the small bag of groceries in the passenger seat of his BMW, searching for the chocolate donut. He promised Autumn he'd lose thirty pounds. Chocolate donuts weren't part of any diet plan he was aware of, but one bite and he'd feel satisfied in some cheap, immediate, and short-lived manner. If only he could isolate the kernel of that artificial comfort and put it in a pill; one with a sugary glaze and a hole in the middle. He'd call it Chocolot, or perhaps Gigglecoca. Sell it in thirteen-pill packs; a baker's dozen. The idea was silly, but he understood fully how silly ideas could make a career.

Seven years earlier, Poultice faced profit losses in the billions as two blockbusters came off patent protection. Simon proposed the "Whimsical Drug Campaign," where previously successful drugs were combined in quirky ways. The result was Coldchol, the antihypertensive and lipid-lowering drug targeted for fast-food eating salesmen; Polarity for both anxiety and erectile dysfunction (the pill, in clown colors, was bent like a hockey stick); and Nicdatsperm, the only drug for both birth control and smoking cessation. The *Wall Street Journal* hailed his revolutionary line of drugs. Poultice promoted him. Since Simon's salary and bonus freed Autumn of income expectations, she withheld judgment.

.   .   .

Simon knew Autumn was sitting in a cracked, hard leather barber chair phoning for information on Trevor Jones and drafting an op-ed piece for the local paper. But what did her good intentions accomplish? Her tireless work with Kids Now earned her many community awards, usually presented at buffet lunches of pasta salads and dried chicken warmed over Sterno. But she couldn't return Trevor Jones to his mother and sisters. Gun violence wouldn't end. He sank into his office chair, buttery leather so soft an air cushion wasn't necessary when his hemorrhoids flared.

"How's the tragedy watch?" he asked Gideon Leaf, his assistant. Simon wanted data. Did a disproportionate number of bad things really happen to good people?

"Fire me," Gideon said, sending a heavy report thumping on Simon's desk. Gideon had mined newspapers, television, and the Internet for victims of sudden, tragic events to ascertain as best he could whether these people were good or bad. His prematurely thin hair was tussled. His sleep-heavy eyes nervously watched Simon run his fingers over brightly colored pie graphs.

"You labeled a huge chunk of pie 'Unfortunate.' What does that mean?"

"Being a teacher, a nurse, or a social worker, doesn't necessarily make a person good. All I can say with absolute certainty is a lot of bad things happen."

Simon shut the binder, asked Gideon to sit. "Focus on drunk drivers," said Simon. "They often escape the awful shit that happens to the poor shmucks they crash into."

Gideon moved restlessly in his chair. "Drunk drivers might have shown poor judgment drinking and driving, but does that necessarily make them bad people?"

Simon sat back, studied his young protégé. "You look like crap."

"I'm a pretty happy guy. But reading all that stuff really bums me out."

Simon smiled. "It should. What are you going to do about it?"

"Go to bed. And stay there."

Simon liked this kid. He graduated with honors from a shitty college and was endlessly trying to prove he belonged with the Ivy League thoroughbreds on his team. Gideon didn't have endless options like the others. Gideon could be trusted.

.   .   .

"Dysluckia isn't a real diagnosis?" Simon said to Gideon. "Ask Trevor Jones."

They were walking outside Poultice Pharmaceuticals, which sat on former wetlands. The formidable steel and dark-windowed building dominated the landscape off the interstate. Deer, wild rabbits, and bird sanctuaries were gone, but the men's loafers kicked along a rutted path audaciously marked as a future nature walk.

"And we might have a treatment."

"You can't just make up a disease," Gideon said, sounding what Simon thought to be abnormally whiny and defiant.

"A few years ago, we studied a promising antihypertensive drug, Tweeta, that fizzled. The trial was done well. Randomized, double blinded. Only the drug proved to be no better than M&Ms in controlling high blood pressure."

"Tweeta? I don't remember it."

"We never got around to publishing the results," said Simon.

"And you can get M&Ms without a prescription."

"I'm serious. Something about the study stuck in my head," said Simon. "Many subjects in the placebo group dropped out due to awful, weird accidents: car wrecks, lightning, electrical fires, even a spontaneous combustion. The Tweeta group escaped such shit luck."

Gideon offered a smile, but remnants of skepticism remained. He raised his face to the sun as if seeking warm licks. "Spring's coming, right?"

"Remember minoxidal, the antihypertensive?" asked Simon. "A side effect, the growth of hair, opened up a huge market. What if Tweeta treats Dysluckia?"

"You need to prove this," said Gideon. "The drug and Dysluckia."

"We will," said Simon. From a distance, the vehicles hurtling at bone-crushing speeds up and down the interstate produced a rhythmic, calming hum. "If the drug works, the disease will cooperate."

.   .   .

Simon told Autumn he had no business going to Trevor Jones's memorial service. He didn't know the kid. But she insisted, and Simon found himself on the south side of town, fearing for his BMW in the church parking lot.

"That's his mom?" Simon said, "She looks young enough to be an older sister."

"And she holds down two jobs, cashier during the week and waitress on weekends," whispered Autumn. "This tragedy will put back some of the years."

Family and friends took turns singing the boy's praises, holding each other upright at the podium. The boy's blighted promise limited their capacity to resist gravity. Trevor's mother asked Autumn to read her op-ed piece. The "amens" from the audience grew in number, gathered energy as she roared to her conclusion.

Trevor Jones fell victim to the part of his life he couldn't control: the violence in which he lived. The bullets that found this poor boy were meant for a convicted felon who remains healthy and free to add to his criminal record. Trevor's neighborhood is darker as a result of his death, and dirtier because of who survived.

Simon pushed himself higher in the back pew. Her voice raged with judgment. Normally opinionated but fair minded, Autumn had transformed before his eyes, as did the crowd. Their grief, isolated and fragile before, galvanized and hardened. The morning sun burned through the stained glass. Through Simon's inspired gaze, the sweating mourners blurred into a washed-out, anonymous glow; the people stuffed into the pews became an ideal community of research subjects.

.   .   .

Simon shopped for dinner. The lemon chicken recipe seemed manageable. He liked lemon only in vodka soda, but lemon chicken reminded him of a sunny chicken, a happy meal, unless you're the chicken. A developmental leap from eggs was necessary, he thought, as Autumn's feverish pitches to funding agencies met empathetic rejections.

Heading to the cashier, he detoured into the bakery aisle to snatch a chocolate donut when his cart crashed into a speeding wheelchair. The young man wore gloves cut at the knuckles, a Muldoon High School sweatshirt.

"Sorry," the young man said. "My brakes are shot." He held a Fosters-sized can, the label calling for donations to support spinal trauma research.

"Are you one of Jerry's kids?" asked Simon.

"People think every young person in a wheelchair belongs to Jerry. Fuck Jerry."

Raw acne screamed out from beneath a tight-fitting hood. Insolent eyebrows arched stiffly. He rattled the can.

Simon admired his grinding jaw. He playfully kicked the rubber wheels, peeled a twenty from his money clip. "Get your brakes fixed."

"Why help people if you're not going to be nice about it?"

Simon puffed a laugh. He imagined Sydney sitting there, then shook his head to erase that thought. "Sorry. My daughter went to Muldoon. Sydney Dunn."

"I know Sydney. Don't worry, we weren't friends," he said, as if reading Simon's expression. "Marching band. I played the clarinet, too."

Simon knew better than to stare at the wheelchair. His eyes locked on the wheels anyway. They didn't seem ideal for marching.

"Legs used to work. A drunk driver ran into my bike."

"You're Roy Milligan," said Simon, remembering his horrible accident before graduation. This was the kid Sydney and her friends visited in the hospital, the kid who the doctors believed might not pull through. "I'm sorry. What shit luck." He gave Roy another twenty.

Roy crumpled the bill in his fist with the first twenty, threw the clump back. Shocked, Simon silently folded the bills neatly into his clip.

"Tell Sydney that Roy says hi," he said, wincing bravely. "It boggles the imagination that she's your daughter. She must take after Mrs. Dunn."

Simon forced a grin, unable to respond. If the comment held a certain degree of truth, could he consider it an insult? He returned to the bakery section. This would be a two-donut drive home.

.   .   .

Simon turned Autumn's desk right-side up, raised the toppled file cabinets. Two police officers walked alongside Autumn as she kicked through a paper blizzard on the floor of Kids Now. Her reflection was split by the cracked wall mirror.

"Is anything missing?" asked an officer. "That you can tell?"

She fought back tears. "I don't know. Obviously someone doesn't like me."

"I know dislike," said Simon, dizzy from all the damage. "There isn't this much clean up after acts of dislike."

"What about enemies?" asked a second officer.

Autumn surveyed the chaos. "I'm feeling woozy," she said.

"No. Definitely not," Simon answered, easing her outside into the morning chill. The sun crouched low on the horizon. He counted more cars in the parking lot than stars in the sky. Loiterers, thought Simon, up to no good. Besides Kids Now, the strip mall contained a card shop, a dollar store, and a nail salon, all of which wouldn't be open for another three hours.

.   .   .

"I have a guess about who trashed the place," Sydney said. She had returned home for spring break and was helping Autumn clean and pack the Kids Now office.

Autumn jumped. "Speak!"

"Your op-ed piece came down real hard on the guy who escaped with a scratch to his ear. Would the neighborhood really be a better place if the bullet killed him?"

"I was angry," Autumn said unapologetically.

"That kind of talk really pisses people off. He's somebody's kid, too. He has a story. Attacking him accomplishes nothing."

Autumn stared out the glass storefront into the parking lot.

"Relax. Nobody's out there," said Sydney, unaware that parked at a distant angle, Simon sat in his car, laptop open, keeping a worried watch. Autumn's banana yellow fleece in the storefront made her a sniper's dream. Burger wrappers and stray fries filled the passenger seat. He had to prove Tweeta treated Dysluckia and soon. First round of layoffs at Poultice were starting. The desperate mood at work only intensified at home. He even considered breaking up a Tweeta pill and hiding it in Autumn's food, except sunny chicken wouldn't camouflage such subterfuge.

That evening Autumn and Simon went to the police, who had already questioned the drug dealer with the scratched ear. "Kids Who?" was his answer. There were no fingerprints. No witnesses. The police weren't surprised. The street honored silence.

.   .   .

Simon feared that honor. Could the responsible person or persons strike closer to home? His neighborhood was too sedate, the stone walls too perfect and high, the old brick Tudors too far from the street, to possess any intimidating street code.

He couldn't sleep. He patrolled the neighborhood in the breezy spring evenings. He considered getting a dog, which thrilled Autumn. A dog would offer protection, peace of mind, an acceptable excuse for skulking around the neighborhood. Simon wasn't a dog person, however. He knew it would sniff out his insecurities in seconds.

Simon checked out suspicious cars, kicked about neighbors' backyards, not really certain what he was looking for. Dewy grass clung to the cuffs of his suit slacks. He wore a suit well; it hid his thirty extra pounds, his man titties. His tailor knew how to translate his width into sturdy authority, even disguise it as muscle.

.   .   .

"Mom told me you're considering med school," Simon said late one night after Sydney returned from the ER, where she was volunteering during spring break.

"Don't know," she said. "The sight of blood makes me sick."

"That could pose a problem," said Simon. The kitchen was dark, lit only by his laptop. He moved papers and folders so she could sit. She hadn't been talking with him much, still shunning him for his role in Poultice's overseas research.

"I'm going to Africa this summer to volunteer at a rural health clinic," she said. "It will be inspiring to be around people dedicated to helping others."

Simon ignored her self-righteous tone. He closed his laptop and smiled. "That's terrific," he said, expecting her to say more. She sipped hot chocolate, slowly chewed a cheese sandwich. "What kind of stuff have you seen in the ER?" asked Simon.

She covered her mouth. "I can't say. Patient confidentiality. It's unethical."

"Ah, yes." Simon grinned. "Unethical."

Simon reminded himself that this was the same little girl who cuddled on his lap as he read *The Velveteen Rabbit.*

"Does it ever bother you that your company makes such huge profits?" asked Sydney. "Yet there are people dying because they can't afford their meds?"

"R&D involves a lot of money and a lot of risk. Why should we apologize when the gamble pays off?" She chewed and sipped, otherwise silent. "Besides, our success pays for your college tuition. Would you prefer to get a job, or take out loans?" he asked. He found vulnerability in her tough gaze, which quickly wilted. "I ran into Roy Milligan recently. He asked about you."

Sydney looked away. "That's nice. He was a nice guy."

"He didn't look past tense to me. He looked like he could use some company."

She hung her head. "Maybe I'll stop by."

"That was a heavy 'maybe,'" he said. "Listen sweetheart, we didn't know if the drugs in those third-world clinical trials would work. We were still testing the side-effect profile. Sometimes the people in the placebo group are the lucky ones. Did you discuss that in your medical ethics class?"

"If the studies were so clean and proper, why didn't you do the trials in the U.S.?"

Simon winced. "I hope you got an A in this course."

"I did." Then, just as when she was little, she abruptly changed subjects, changed moods, and moved on. "Tonight someone dropped off a gunshot victim. Pop, pop, pop. Three times in the groin."

She smiled at his discomfort.

"The doctors were certain they'd find serious damage. The groin is packed tight with important stuff. Major blood vessels, nerves, the bladder, the family jewels." A lustrous gleam filled her face. "The bullets missed everything."

"Lucky dude, huh?"

"The police thought this was payback. He'd allegedly raped a friend's sister. The guy was cursing and spitting, a real creep. The doctors said this happens all the time. If he'd been a decent guy, he'd probably be dead."

Simon turned on his laptop and started typing.

"This is confidential stuff."

Simon mimed locking his lips and swallowing the key.

"How can you swallow the key *after* you've locked your mouth?"

.   .   .

Simon found an abandoned movie theater at the edge of town. A planned renovation had ceased for unknown reasons years before. Simon stood captivated on the balcony beside Gideon, who couldn't stop coughing. Mildew and buttered popcorn thickened the air. Gold tassels tied the voluptuous burgundy curtains to the sides of the ripped movie screen. Many houselights were blown. "It's perfect," Simon said.

Gideon's face was pale. He felt sick. "You can't be serious."

.   .   .

The Poultice Executive Committee nodded soberly as Simon spoke.

"Two study groups comprising good and bad people, arranged randomly, will stand in a movie theater. Half have taken Tweeta; half only sugar pills. Three blindfolded hires will direct bullets from the balcony above and we'll assess the resultant damage."

Simon expected the gasps, the pale faces. After all, his colleagues rightfully considered themselves good people.

"The subjects will be protected," said Simon. "To a degree."

"Do the folks in legal know about this?" asked Dick Levy.

Incredulous whispers about the safety of research subjects echoed later in the bathroom. During the meeting, however, not a single dissenting voice was heard. A second round of layoffs was expected by year's end, and this drug had people excited. A new drug for a new disease spelled blockbuster. Wellbourne was caught dancing in his office. The name of the new drug? Fortunata.

.   .   .

Gideon darkened the celebratory mood, insisting that all subjects be protected head to toe by state-of-the-art armor. "What are you doing?" Simon asked. "You're on our team. We agreed on riot helmets, bulletproof vests to cover chest and back."

"Hard armor or soft armor?" asked Gideon, using PowerPoint to list the merits and limitations of KEVLAR, VECTRAN, and Biosteel, spider silk twenty times stronger than a similar strain of steel.

"Counting bullet holes in armor isn't enough. We need suitable risk exposure," said Simon. "Location can't predict penetration." People squirmed in their seats. "C'mon folks," Simon pressed forward. He retold Sydney's ER story. "Swiss cheese groin, and the guy's back, spanking the monkey in days. Harm is necessary. It's a measure of outcome."

The legal people insisted on full protection, head to toe, or no study.

"Exactly," said Gideon, staring at his pen. "Isn't this the 'saving lives' business?"

"Fine," said Simon, sour-faced, hurt. "Don't think you can make omelets without breaking a few eggs."

.   .   .

This setback didn't temper Simon's excitement when one hundred people, geared up like blindfolded riot police, were escorted into the decrepit theater. From a microphone near the screen he informed them again about what was about to happen. "You'll be exposed to ten seconds of low-level weaponry from three blindfolded hires. One will be shooting blanks," he said, pointing to the balcony behind and above them. "Half of you have been taking the study drug for a month, the other half a sugar pill. We don't know who has been taking what. Only you know if you've been naughty or nice."

Good and *Bad* people were recruited by a contract group expert in such work. They agreed with Simon and Gideon; such judgments were subjective at best. Surprises abound. Screening ex-cons for the *Bad* group, they discovered classic sufferers of Dysluckia who qualified for the study as part of the *Good* group.

Each person received five thousand dollars. Fair compensation, Simon thought, for ten seconds of work. As well as limited health coverage for injuries resulting directly from the study.

.   .   .

Screams. Diving and colliding bodies. Simon stood in the balcony, mesmerized, horrified, and rejoicing in his accomplishment. Ten seconds. The gunfire wasn't stopping. He distracted himself. What if Sydney found out about this? How would he find a way into an explanation? Maybe later, when much older and seasoned from making complicated choices herself, she might permit understanding. He wasn't as concerned with Autumn. She had lost threads in her idealism. She wouldn't approve, or understand, but like the ugly birthday sweater Sydney once got for her, she'd wear it stoically.

Gideon stood beside him, eyes narrowed, tears pouring down his fine features. "They're fully protected," Simon yelled to assure him, unable to hear his own voice. The gunfire stopped. Only screams remained, and gun smoke fog resembling dust in projector light. The chaos below could be the climactic scene in any blockbuster, where heroes and villains are clearly identified, the ending hopeful and satisfying. But it wasn't.

Gideon couldn't release his grip from the balcony rail. He stood motionless, ossified, wiped clean of emotion.

.   .   .

Private ambulances lined up behind the theater, alongside dumpsters still brimming with demolition from the renovation that never was. Inside the

Simon now realized Kids Now wasn't a job, a career, or a passion; it was a grand moral gesture, an apology for their comfortable life, their brick house, and his work.

Simon was promoted, lavished with a fat bonus, and slightly ashamed with how easily it was attained. Gideon refused the money and resigned, mumbling something about divinity school. "Go, if you want to do God's work," Simon told him, "but if you want to do work that God wished he could do, you'll stay."

The academic year was closing and Sydney was busy packing for a summer trip to Italy and France, where studying art history sounded better than malaria and HIV in the bush.

"Mom knows something," she said to Simon. "About the study."

"Something or everything?"

"I didn't say a word." She made the motion of locking her lips. "But I found a draft of an article on the computer."

"Not another op-ed piece?" Simon said, as if a debilitating disease had returned.

.　　.　　.

Poultice beefed up its legal department to fend off inquiries prompted by publication of the study. But medical progress was built on exploitations in medical research, and instead of punishment, many of these investigators were bestowed with the highest honors. Legal concerns didn't bother Simon. He considered all critics future customers.

.　　.　　.

Mrs. Jones stopped by to visit with Autumn. She could finally breathe without pain and was gaining strength, which she'd need to find work. Her bosses at the cashier and waitressing jobs both sent cards when she was hospitalized, then hired other people to take her place.

Autumn stared blank-eyed over her garden, effusively in bloom. "I wish I could help," she said, cutting a rose, painstakingly snipping the thorns. "This is all I have to give you."

Mrs. Jones smiled, buried her nose into the petals. "It's enough. For now." She squeezed Autumn's hand. "You OK?" she asked.

Autumn wiped soil and sweat from her face. "I am."

Simon met up with Mrs. Jones at her car. "How you doing?"

Mrs. Jones flexed her arm and made a muscle.

"The study was a good thing, right?" Simon asked.

"Of course. I'm five thousand dollars richer."

"And a greater good will come from it."

"Trevor was shot for no reason at all," she said. "I can't leave the house, or sit by the living room window, without thinking about when the next bullet is coming. You paid me very well for a risk I take every day for free."

"If Trevor had taken Fortunata, maybe *he'd* have the ear abrasion," said Simon.

Mrs. Jones looked defeated. "Then someone else, some poor child just as nice and innocent, but not taking the drug, would be a victim."

.   .   .

On Simon's suggestion, Dick Levy approached Autumn about directing the new South Side clinic.

"The people in this neighborhood need access to good doctors," said Levy.

"You mean doctors who prescribe Fortunata," said Autumn.

"They deserve the best health care," said Levy. "We can provide that."

Autumn swirled her bourbon, staring into it as if it might divine an answer. "I'll think about it."

"Good." Levy clapped his hands. "Only don't think too hard."

.   .   .

That night, after Sydney called from Nice, buoyant, asking if she sounded tan, Autumn kissed Simon on the cheek and headed to bed.

"I worry about you, Simon," she said, stopping on the stairs.

Simon tried to respond. He pulled off his tie, worked it in his hands, wishing words handled as easily as silk. "Take a walk with me?" he said.

She broke into a plaintive smile.

They strolled the sidewalk hand in hand. Simon wanted to take this starlit sky and wrap it snugly over her shoulders, now peeling from too much sun, when an explosion jolted the quiet night. A backfiring car probably, but Autumn jumped, and Simon groped her from head to toe, toe to head, feeling for bullet wounds.

"What are you doing, Simon? You're hurting me," she giggled. "Stop it."

Assured she wasn't injured, he crushed her with a hug. It had been a long time since they seriously held each other. An icy tightness seized his chest. What was this feeling? Not pain. He couldn't take a finger and point to its location. It was vague, unidentifiable, and terrifying. Simon looked up and down the now quiet street.

"What's wrong?" asked Autumn.

"I'm not a good person," he said with relief, thinking about bad things happening to good people. The study didn't confirm that. But the lack of objective data didn't ease Simon's fears. The world can be cruel, the imagination, too.

13

Calling the Code

The physician sweeps a final, downcast eye over the body tucked between white sheets. Silver hair combed into a sharp part. Aftershave lingering in the lamplight. Stubborn traces of life that sting the physician. The man had plans that evening, had been well enough to care about style, the physician thinks, holding onto a deep, unsatisfying breath. Now he must call the next of kin. The only phone number belongs to the man's sister. When she answers, he reveals only that her brother is in the emergency department and he's critically ill. A chilled silence follows, but words are accumulating meaning, gaining a charge. The physician braces for a storm of grief. "I need to find a ride. The legs don't work too good," the sister finally says, unexpectedly calm.

The physician sighs sweet relief. "Take your time. We'll wait."

Nurses close off the room. The emergency department teems with life, making it a more charitable space for viewing the body than the sterile tranquility of the basement morgue. The physician scrambles to catch up with the many patients lost on his radar during the long code. He's also haunted by the horde of people camping in the waiting room for a bed.

An hour later she calls back. "How is he?"

Deceit aches. The physician bites his tongue. The years have taught him that news of sudden death demands intimacy, awkward and ill fitting as it may be. Over the phone it can feel like bumping against a darkness where some objects are fragile and others wired with explosives.

"It would be easier if we can talk face to face," he says.

"I'm on my way. Please tell him that?"

"Sure," he says, rubbing beneath the sweat-stained neck of his scrub top. Manifesting a breezy tone is stressful when the very condition for the conversation is bad news, where words pass through a filter of self-doubt and second-guessing, grind against alternative treatments, even crazy ones; this is what the wounded ego feeds on in its efforts to pretend a better outcome and an easier discussion.

Another hour passes. "I just spoke to the sister," says the social worker, his voice sinking. "No ride."

"Seriously? She can't call a cab?"

The social worker removes his glasses, blows fog to clean the lenses. "You have no other choice."

The physician drops his chin to his chest, still tight from the failed resuscitation. Decisions weren't so much made as options eliminated. "The code cart is empty," a younger physician finally joked, "No meds left," which softened the strain and frustration in the nurses' faces, but not by much. The code had gone on way too long, he knew that, but he couldn't find that sense of an ending, recognize when enough is enough, or even worse, when enough is too much. Then he caught sight of the medical student lost in the brutish chore of chest compressions, sweat limping off his forehead and onto the patient. The student was exhausted, or maybe sick from the realization that the crunching beneath his thrusts were cracking ribs. "Breaking bones is part of CPR done well," the physician told the student. "Hope and bruising often come in the same package."

The physician calls back, breaks the news. He believes he can trace the sister's tears by her gulping breaths. He even reaches for a box of tissues. A bystander might suspect he's consoling the slow and outdated computer. "Again, I'm sorry for your loss." The physician can't figure out whether the sister needs space to cry or feels abandoned in anticipation for more details. Or maybe she hung up, disappointed and disrespected by his audacity. He had lied to her.

"Hello?" the physician says.

The clumsiness of the scene is complicated by the TV blasting in the background at her home.

"Hello?"

"My son isn't very considerate," the sister says.

An angry voice rips through the canned television laughter, tells her to be quiet. It belongs to a man who probably owns a car, the physician believes, or could steal one if he needed to.

"Can you hear me?" she says.

"I'm sorry? Are you speaking to me?" says the physician.

"Who else would I be talking to?"

"Maybe your son . . ."

"I've wasted enough breaths on him." Sniffling mists the phone line. "Where's he at? My brother?"

"The ER. His body. Thinking it was best for you to see him . . ."

"You lied to me," she interrupts. "He was dead when you first called me, wasn't he?"

"Giving the news over the phone can be dangerous. Sometimes folks become very upset. They dash to the hospital and crash and become patients themselves. We try to avoid that."

"I don't drive. I can't."

"Yes, you told me." The physician squeezes the receiver, nestles against it, then pulls away. It stinks of ear sweat and cheap plastic. "Your brother called 911 himself. The medics said he was breathing when they found him on the floor of his apartment."

"He kept that place spotless," she says. "Not much need for furniture, except for that futon. Who can get up from those things?"

"Your brother's heart stopped in the ambulance. The medics were all over it."

"What makes you think I want to hear all this?"

"The chain of events were lined up just so. I thought we could save him. We tried everything."

The explosions from the TV float over the physician.

"He had a heart attack a few weeks ago," the sister says. "You knew that, right? A small one."

He hears the ping of gunfire, hollering and music throbbing with faux suspense.

"What's this?"

"Can you hear me?"

The physician forces the phone against his ear.

"He walked out of a hospital in Connecticut. His heart had blockages, the doctors said. Next day, he's back on the site lugging rebar."

"Say again?"

"He didn't have medical. He never bought a stitch if he didn't have the cash in his pocket. He was responsible in that way. I told him to stop being stupid. He said the hospital bills would kill him before any heart attack."

"He knew he might die?"

"It had to be on his mind, right?" she says.

This news shouldn't diminish the tragedy, but the physician feels a smile, a reprieve from responsibility, slipping into his face. The distance from the sister now offers refuge. "Can you lower the sound?" the physician asks, aware that it's *her* home. "Maybe go into another room?"

"It's a landline," she says. "The cord only stretches so far."

The physician remembers what she had said earlier, that she didn't walk too well.

"You need to show some respect," she says.

"Excuse me?"

"Not you." She appeals to her son. "My brother just died. Please."

The television sounds recede.

"That's better. You were saying, doctor?"

"I'm sorry," the physician says.

"You already said that. Doesn't matter anyway. I was hoping . . ."

"What's that?" the physician says.

"I wanted to see him," she says, her voice crumbling. The wave of television noise slowly rising.

"Doesn't your son drive? Have a car?"

"He does. He does. But he's very busy. It's better this way. He and his uncle didn't see eye to eye. We weren't close."

"Put your son on the line," the physician says.

"Nothing good would come of that," she says.

The physician wants to argue, except he has not earned the right. He couldn't save her brother. What's left is an irrational need to rescue, or at least salvage, this conversation.

"Don't you want to say goodbye?" says the physician. "Closure is important."

"You know, I was once an excellent driver."

Shrieking tires peel through the phone line. The physician listens for the sister's voice. "Mrs.—?" The physician doesn't remember her name. He knows her only as the sister of the deceased, the next of kin who needed to be notified. "Hello?" Enough bad television dialogue. The longer he waits the sillier he feels. Silliness sharpens into anger, then anger morphs into doubt. Should he be concerned for her safety, calling the police? No. Enough with the crashing vehicles, the insane whoops. *What are you doing,* he presses himself. Hanging on the line, abandoned by logic, he sees himself in the moment and looking back on it, an illusionary hindsight that offers no answers, but carries no regrets either. *Enough,* he tells himself, *you did your best; enough,* and returns the phone to its cradle.